I0588840

THE ARCHEOLOGIST

EVELYN ASTRA

© Evelyn Astra

Evelyn Astra asserts the moral right to be identified as the author of this work.

This novel is entirely a work of fiction. The names, characters, and incidents portrayed in it are the work of the author's imagination. Any resemblance to actual persons, living or dead, events or localities is entirely coincidental.

Evelyn Astra
@evelyn_astra_author on Instagram
astraevelyn1@gmail.com

Dedicated to AT: my love, my inspiration, and my biggest supporter. This book wouldn't exist without you.

Also to my grandma, for always believing in me - please don't read this.

Table of Contents

"I CAN BE A PERFECT GENTLEMAN WHEN WARRANTED... YOU WARRANT PERFECT. AND A GENTLEMAN."

Alexander Turner is a gorgeous millionaire, and boy does he know it. Having turned his day job as an archeologist into a lucrative start up, he spends his days travelling, collecting artefacts, then selling them - this time to fund a mysterious new venture.

When he meets a gorgeous stranger at one of his auctions, his world is quickly shaken - along with his long-standing conviction to never have a relationship longer than a one night stand.

***

Nefertari Garcia is still new to the art curatorship scene, but her exhibitions have helped her aunt's museum climb the social ladder. Looking for a one-in-a-million
piece for her first solo exhibit - and the museum's final
one before it's sold - she never expected to meet anyone. Especially not a man who looks like one of her Greek statues...

As Xander and Nef's relationship gets hot and heavy, so do the challenges that stand in their way. Xander has a secret, one that might just break Nef's heart.

Will their love story become mythology written in the stars? Or will they become ancient history?

Content Advisory:

This book contains minor depictions of violence (chapter 14) and male SASH (no violence, groping; chapter 19).

CHAPTER 1

Jurassic Park had nothing on him. After three months of non-stop directing, digging, and negotiations, Alexander was finally one step away from securing his next big project. And god was it an expensive one, currently overseen by a woman scarier than any T-Rex Jeff Goldblum had narrowly escaped. Waving away the red sand that seemed to permanently sting his eyes, Xander jogged towards the beat-up jeep where his friend and colleague Asim waited in the drivers seat.

"It's in good condition!" Xander shouted over the wind. White shirt flapping, he hauled himself into the passenger seat. It was easier to talk in the confines of the car. "We don't know which Pharaoh it depicts yet, but the bust seems to be undamaged."

The bust was incredible. Perfectly preserved by the hot dry sands, some colour even remained to give the eyes and clothing depicted life. A seasoned collector and Egyptology enthusiast, Alexander had known the second he laid eyes on it that it would be the prize of his collection. A shame that the collection was planning to be sold that very night, at a ball to raise funds for his upcoming project.

Asim grunted his approval. A quiet man with dark eyes, he was reliable — as a friend and employee. He had been working with Alexander for as long as he could remember; a stoic, silent companion who somehow had a knack for knowing exactly where to dig to find the best relics. Clapping his arm on Asim's shoulder, Xander grinned.

"This piece will be perfect. Once it's identified we can grab a final price and then make that offer we've been talking about."

Another grunt, this time a bit more enthusiastic. Xander and Asim had been planning on selling their collection for months now. Finding enough pieces to reach their budget had been challenging, but with a steady team and persistence they had slowly reached their goal. Over their goal, if tonight went well. Backing slowly out of the site, careful to avoid the men in similar loose linen shirts and dusty trousers, the pair headed back to their hotel.

Located on the shore of the Nile, the Ra rose out of the dust streaked sky. Lights glimmered in the rows of windows, uniformed men dashed in and out of the reception, and all around was the sound of Arabic and blaring car horns. Alexander sat quietly through it all, thinking about the evening ahead.

The ball would start promptly at seven. He had invited the most prominent art collectors he knew, and several more he didn't. A handful of curators, art critics, and members of the Egyptian government would also be present, along with (unfortunately) a representative of the British Museum. While the goal was to sell as much of his long-amassed collection of artifacts and art to raise funds for a new project, Alexander felt passionately enough about supporting small business that he had also invited some lesser known collectors to join.

In order to promote his pieces, he had also hired a professional curator to set up an exhibition in the Grand Ballroom, for guests to wander through both before and after the sit down dinner.

It felt strange knowing his pieces would soon be on display. Where they had normally sat decorating his home in San Diego, little representations of his passions, his life's work, they had now been lovingly wrapped, packaged, and shipped all the way across the world to be ogled and sold to strangers. How ironic that in his desire to have his own museum, he would have to give up his collection to fund it.

Strolling through the lobby, Xander debated peeking at the exhibition currently still being set up. The curator, Grace, was standing just inside the doorway of the ballroom speaking rapidly in Italian as she coordinated her team.

"Ancora due ore gente, MUOVIAMOCI! L'illuminazione deve essere perfetta, oh Issy, move that bust to the left a bit..." Trailing off into English, Grace spotted Alexander and shot him a long lashed glare. Snapping her red nails in his face, she berated him.

"It is not ready! Do not look or you will rush me, and then quindi aiutami Dio. When will you send me that bust you found? I need the main piece so I can get the lighting right."

Not waiting for his response, Grace spotted someone across the lobby and dashed away, presumably to find that bust he had been so excited to tell Asim about earlier. Deciding against angering her, Alexander left the ballroom to be a surprise and instead took the lift up to his suite.

Finally, he thought. Removing his shoes, he paused by the windows to look at the skyline across the Nile. Reflection sparkling on the river, the view followed Alexander into the tiled bathroom, where a large bath stood opposite a double basin vanity. Ignoring the bath, Xander watched himself strip in the large mirror.

Unbuttoning the sleeves at his elbows, he pulled the soft shirt away and dropped it into the laundry basket he had brought with him. His dark auburn hair fell in layers to his jaw, and his matching beard was scruffy from neglecting it during the last few days of the dig. Piercing blue eyes stared back at him and he stretched down to remove his pants, abs flexing.

The shower in the corner was large, and Alexander sighed as he washed off the day's dirt. As much as he loved a good day's hard work, he did enjoy the various events he attended throughout the year — specifically the opportunity to not appear like he lived in the wild most of his life. After all, he was a highly respected, wealthy business man.

And tonight, it was most important he looked the part.

Nef thought she looked pretty good, considering she had only finished a 17 hour flight that morning. Sleeping pills definitely had something to do with it, along with the last few hours of having her skin buffed to perfection, her nails painted a deep red, and finding a hair product that finally held her dark curls in perfect bouncing spirals.

Tonight was important. Tonight, she needed to make an Impression. Tonight, she was going to put her budget to good use and was going to outbid a room full of seasoned collectors for as many pieces she could possibly afford for her exhibition for Aunt Tiye.

Nef felt a pang at the thought of her aunt. Owner of a museum in San Diego, Nef had been working for Aunt Tiye since she was a teen. From handling the tickets at the front desk to her role as a tour guide, Nef had eventually taken on the role of art historian and curator once she graduated from college. It was just a shame her first proper exhibition would be the museum's final one, before it was sold to some anonymous buyer.

As if Tiye had known she was thinking of her, Nef's phone buzzed loudly from the small kitchenette in her hotel room at the Ra in Cairo.

"Dearest!" Tiye's voice tinkled out of the phone, her strong American accent belying her Egyptian heritage. Tiye had immigrated to America in the forties where she had met Sebastian Garcia Perez, and hadn't left his side since.

"Aunty T!" Just hearing her voice helped settle the butterflies in Nef's stomach.

"Put me on video, my love, let me look at you. I can feel your nerves from here."

Nef obliged, and propped the phone up against the wide bathroom mirror as she started to apply her eyeliner. Tiye's squeal of approval made her quickly turn down the phone's volume.

"I TOLD you that dress was perfect! You look so grown up, so professional! A force to be reckoned with, my little Magpie."

Grinning at the endearment — gifted to her for her love of all things shiny — Nef tried to see herself from

Tiye's perspective. Her hair was out in all its curly glory, spiralling in layers just to below her collar bones. Her black-coffee eyes were rimmed with black liner, and she deftly applied her signature red lipstick to match her nails.

Stepping back a bit, Nef eyed her snug curves, wrapped tightly in sheer black chiffon from the high necked halter neckline to the waist, before becoming more opaque as the skirt flared down to brush the floor. Her black stilettos were just high enough to prevent her from tripping on the hem, and her stick on bra blended in with her skin enough so that it wasn't noticeable through the sheer material — she envied those smaller-breasted girls who could go without. She looked... she looked like a woman ready to fight for those art pieces.

"How are you feeling little Magpie?" Tiye's voice interrupted her thoughts.

"Feeling ready, Aunty T. I've got my list of preferred pieces, plus any backups in case I can't afford the main ones."

"Don't you worry about affording anything dearest, you just bid and win and I'll work out the rest. I want only the best for this exhibition." A tinge of sadness had entered Tiye's voice then, an acknowledgement that although this exhibition would be Nef's pride and joy, the kickstarter to her career, it would be the last of Tiye's life's work.

Pushing past the sudden lump in her throat, Nef smiled at her aunt. "I promise I won't worry then."

Tiye visibly relaxed, and Nef hadn't realised how stressed she was until she also let out her breath. Grabbing her clutch and keycard, Nef was ready to say goodbye but Tiye had started speaking again.

"Have you met the host yet, love?" There was something off in Tiye's tone, but the question distracted her.

"Not yet. I assume I'll meet him tonight, apparently he usually gives a speech at these events. Is there anything you wanted me to ask him?"

Tiye opened her mouth, then closed it again. "No dearest, just excited for you to meet someone with an equally strong passion for curatorship. I've heard rumours his exhibition tonight is supposed to be… extravagant to say the least."

"I'll send you photos."

"You better, little Magpie. Now go make some bids!"

Exchanging goodbyes and good lucks, Nef finally hung up and made her way to the lobby. Mention of her host's exhibition reminded her of her second purpose here: to find and befriend whoever curated tonight. Maybe the curator had a job opening… goodness knows Nef needed one after the year was up.

Reaching the ballroom, Nef brushed down her dress once more and took a deep breath. It was time to start working.

CHAPTER 2

The ballroom was perfect. Dimly lit with hanging lanterns, clusters of candles, and well placed hidden lights, heavy drapes blocking the floor to ceiling view of the Nile on the left, sandstone pillars had been strategically placed throughout the marble floor and columns. On each pillar, a bust, artifact, or scroll had been lovingly placed, some secured behind glass boxes, others open for guests to closely crowd around.

Alexander smiled politely to everyone has he made his way through his faux museum. Subtly scratching his neck, he adjusted his deep red tie, the only splash of colour on his otherwise midnight black suit. Even his cufflinks, shaped to mimic the bust of Nefertiti, were black metal.

A podium had been set up at the far end of the hall, with an arrangement of tables and chairs in front of it. Uniformed waiters stood quietly to the side, by a hidden door leading to the kitchens. Checking that the name tags were set at each seat, Xander finally allowed himself to relax a bit. So far, everything looked exactly as he had designed. Now it was time for everything to go exactly as planned. A hand suddenly clapped down on his shoulder.

"This is perfect, my friend," Asim said. Decked in a dashing tuxedo, with his dark skin and long lashes, Asim looked like he had stepped out of a perfume ad. From the stares he was drawing from some nearby women, Asim probably knew it too.

"Will you mingle tonight, or try keep your illusion of mystery?"

Xander chuckled softly. "I thought the ladies liked my 'illusion of mystery'," he quipped.

"Not that you have been seeing any ladies lately, eh?" Asim gave his friend a knowing stare. "How long has it been since you let yourself have a good night? You know any of these women — or men, for that matter — would kill for some of your attention."

"Attention, yes..." Xander agreed quietly. Unfortunately, it was true. He was no prude, and he knew he was considered an attractive man. And there were definitely some women catching his eye tonight.

But his first few relationships had all crashed and burned when they realised he loved his archeology more than them. Ever since, Xander had a strict one-night-only policy. They don't get lead on, he gets what he wants. Win-win. By the way some of the guests were eying him, they had heard about said policy — and looked interested.

A delicate blonde in a white silk gown teased at her dress strap with a knowing smile. Xander gave a matching grin, and was about to head over to talk to her when his watch beeped.

7:30pm. Time to start. Alexander made his way to the podium, nodded to one of the hotel employees, and the lights somehow dimmed further until he was left spotlit on the stage.

"Good evening, everyone. Thank you for joining me here tonight." His deep voice rang out through the hall, and guests started gathering closer. "If you would all please find your seats, entrees will be served promptly. We will then have our auction, before mains are served."

A few murmurs of excitement at that. Xander continued, a small well rehearsed speech about the significance of many of the objects on display — and their value. A hopeful attempt to whet his audience's appetite further.

"I hope you all found the pieces you are looking for in the hall. Good luck with the auction, and enjoy your meal."

Applause rang out as Xander stepped back from the microphone. As he did, he glanced up over the crowd, slowly dispersing to their seats. Something, no, *someone*, caught his eye.

All Xander saw was a flash of red lips and dark eyes before she turned away to find her seat, curls bouncing with every step. A backless, black dress hugged her generous curves, and Xander realised he was staring blatantly at her ass. Shaking himself slightly, Xander made a mental note to find this woman later. For now, he made his way to his seat by Asim, finally ready for the auction.

Wow, Nef thought as she made her way to her seat. She had been a bit slow to drag her eyes away from the host, and now hurried so she wouldn't be the last one standing. He had been the most attractive man she had ever seen in her life. Broad shoulders in a fitted suit, neatly trimmed beard that she wouldn't mind scraping her skin as she —

She dropped heavily into her seat as she found her name tag, and smiled at the others on her table. Hopefully her cheeks weren't too flushed. Entrees were already being delivered to each guest, and introductions were quickly made as they dug in.

One one side of Nef, Lydia, a stern, regal looking black woman who had been collecting art for years ("I usually prefer Roman mosaics but I've always loved Alexander's work") was arguing with her seat neighbour about a particular scroll they had seen earlier, and was waving her arms to the point her drink was in danger of spilling. On her other side David, a middle aged bespectacled man, was trying to talk to Hannah, a beautiful blonde in a white silk dress at least half his age. This seemed the safer conversation option for the moment.

"David, was it?" Nef lightly tapped his shoulder to get his attention, and Hannah flashed her a grateful smile. "What pieces are you most interested in tonight?"

David's eyes widened when he took Nef in, but she clenched her fists around her cutlery and avoided shifting in her seat.

"Obviously, I'm most interested in that main bust. I'm sure it'll go for quite a price. I can afford it, of course," he continued with an air of condescension. "Besides, Alexander and I are old friends, I'm sure he'll appreciate my input in tonight's events. But you, I've never seen you before, and I've attended every ball the man has hosted! What's your story?"

It was Nef's turn to flash Hannah a sympathetic grimace. David, fortunately, didn't seem to notice.

"I'm Nef —" she started.

"Nef? As in Nefertiti?" David looked delighted. Holding in a sigh, Nef shook her head.

"As in Nefertari, the wife of Ramses the Great. All the women in my family are named after Egyptian queens."

David and Hannah looked impressed. "Well, Nef, what brings you to one of these events? Are you here on someone's behalf? Representing a museum perhaps?"

"I'm a curator from San Diego. I'm designing an exhibition for a museum and wanted to find some pieces for it." Nef left out the it was her aunt's museum — nepotism was not something she felt a need to discuss with David. Besides, she was a good curator. She may not have directed her own exhibition before, but she had planned and designed almost all of her aunt's since, and it was the museum's success that had garnered interest in it being bought.

"And what pieces are you interested in dear?"

Bristling at the unwarranted endearment, Nef held her chin high. She had already known exactly which pieces she wanted, and it was time to not be shy about it.

"Well obviously, that main bust is a masterpiece. I have to have it. There are a few others, but I'm sure I can find similar styles elsewhere if tonight doesn't work out."

Lydia chuckled, argument apparently over. "You have competition, David!" She called across the table. David scowled.

"Me and everyone else in here who wants that bust. Besides, Alexander is one of the luckiest archeologists in this age — no-one finds what he finds. You won't see anything like this collection ever again sweetheart.

Tonight's your best chance. Good luck." David turned back to Hannah, a clear dismissal.

Unfortunately, Nef knew David was right. She would never find a collection this exquisite again. Fortunately, she had come prepared to fight.

Alexander cleared his throat and took a sip of water from a cup by the podium. The auction was almost over, and it had already made him a large profit. Asim was grinning over his drink, arm slung around an attractive girl in a red dress that he had been flirting with all night. From the way she kept shifting closer to him, Xander knew he wouldn't see his friend until the next day once tonight ended.

It was time for the final auction of the night, the one everyone had been waiting for. Greedy eyes stared back at him from every table. Sweeping the room, he stopped when he found the girl in the black dress. Her red lips were set in a small smile, as though she knew a secret no one else did. He had been surprised when she had bid (and won) earlier — on a small scrap of papyrus depicting Osiris and Anubis. He hadn't thought she would be a collector. Which was stupid, considering the majority of his guests were.

Xander cleared his throat again. Here he was, making stupid assumptions about a woman when he knew damn well appearances weren't everything. She looked to be a similar age to him, and while they both seemed relatively young, age did not mean anything when it came to appreciating history. Besides, right now was not the time to be thinking about women at all. Or what her red lips made him think of.

"We now have the final piece up for auction. I know you have all been waiting for this. Tonight, I present the star of my collection, the death mask of Queen Thuya, wife of Yuya."

As Xander spoke, four men carefully brought the mask onto the stage. Larger than a normal head, the solid gold mask was detailed enough the the hair strands were visible from the back row of the tables — naturally planned by Grace, to ensure maximum wow factor. The chest plate's turquoise, navy blue, and rust red painted geographical shapes sparkled in the warm lighting. Parts of the gold had been blackened by age, but Xander thought that only increased the appeal of the bust. The eyes retained their paint. Lined in blue, they seemed to stare down the audience, daring someone to start bidding.

"The price starts at two million USD."

The hall erupted. Bidding cards flashed from all over the hall, ridiculous sums called out in an effort to win the mask.

The first three minutes went by in a blur as the price was driven higher and higher, until only three bidders were left. David, red-faced and sweating, Juan, a Columbian retail mogul who sporadically showed up to

Xander's events, and the girl in the black dress, still lightly smiling with those infuriatingly distracting lips. At least he was staring at her face this time, though keeping his eyes level was an effort.

Slightly ashamed of how he was objectifying this unknown woman, Xander took another sip of water before continuing the auction. The price now stood at nearly five million USD. Enough to fund his next project with spare. The thrill of victory settling inside him, he asked the remaining bidders if they wanted to keep going.

"Six million!" David suddenly called, sounding breathless. He glanced angrily towards the girl in black, who remained calm and poised.

"Bah, I'm out." Juan dropped his bidding card on the table and downed his champagne.

"6.1 million." The woman's voice rang out calmly, and David swiped at his brow.

"6.2 million," he responded.

"6.5 million," the woman countered.

The hall was silent. This was an incredible sum of money. How did she have this much? Who was she? Alexander was certain he would have remembered if he has seen her at any of his other events.

"David?" Xander called. "6.5 million. Would you like to raise?"

Whispers broke out as David wiped his brow again. He downed his drink and wiped his brow once more.

The woman continued to sit calmly, smile growing slightly.

"I'm out." He finally muttered. The woman's smile widened.

"David is out." Xander confirmed. "6.5 million USD for Queen Thuya's gold death mask, to the woman in black." He felt himself flush slightly for calling her that out loud. "Going once, going twice…"

Her smile turned into a victorious grin, and he thought it might just be the most beautiful smile he had ever seen.

"Gone!"

CHAPTER 3

The woman in the black dress stood in front of Thuya's death mask, back on its podium and lit from beneath. Alexander stopped just behind her, close enough to smell her citrus and vanilla perfume. Trying not to visibly breathe in deeply, Xander spoke quietly.

"Congratulations," he rumbled. "That was quite a show you gave everyone."

The woman turned towards him, and he didn't need to try to breathe slowly because his breath completely stopped. She was easily the most beautiful woman he had seen. Generous curves hidden beneath tight black material, an air of maturity and elegance, and those damn red lips. He wanted to fist her curls in his hands while she took him deep down her throat.

"Thank you," she said, lips curving into a smile. "You have an incredible collection."

Her voice wasn't doing anything to help his growing arousal. Rich and smooth, with a slight accent. He wanted to hear her moan his name.

What the fuck was wrong with him? He always found someone to take home at events like these (once multiple someones) but he had never been so instantly turned on to the point he reverted back to his teenage self. This was supposed to be a professional event, damnit. Shaking himself mentally, he held out a hand.

"I'm Alexander, but my friends call me Xander."

"I'm Nef." Nef smiled up at him, taking his hand in a solid shake.

"Nef." Xander savoured the feel of her name on his tongue. Wanted something else on his tongue. "Short for anything?"

"Yes, but I'll leave you to guess what."

Was she flirting with him? He wanted to know her full name now. He wanted to know a lot of things about her. But most appropriately for now, he wanted to know

"How long have you been collecting?"

Nef laughed, another sound that shot straight to Xander's cock.

"I'm no collector," she said. "Although these guests of yours might murder me for it. I'm an art curator, I work for a museum in San Diego."

Impressive. A museum in San Diego… maybe he knew which one?

"Must be some museum," Xander murmured, "to be able to afford $6.5 million for a bust."

"Oh it is. Although my exhibition will be its final hurrah I'm afraid." Nef's eyes grew dark, and Xander could have kicked himself for making this woman anything other than happy.

"I would love to see your exhibition," he said, trying to get her mind off whatever the end of this museum meant to her. Nef perked back up, a grin lighting up her face.

"I promise it will be worth it. And considering that your mask will be the star of the show, you have to come. I'll send you an invite."

A thrill shot through his stomach. She'd send him an invite. Idiot, he thought to himself. Just learnt her name and now he's getting excited like a schoolboy with a crush. Still, the thought of seeing her more than just once made him feel…excited, for the first time in a while.

"I'd love that," Xander purred. "But it is your mask now, not mine. I would love to hear more about your exhibition though. I'm about to go play host some more, but would you like to come with me tomorrow to the dig? There might be some more items you'd like for it."

Nef seemed startled by the invitation. Worried he might have been too forward, he opened his mouth to retract the statement somehow, but Nef spoke first.

"I'd love to!" The genuine happiness in her eyes satisfied him.

"Good. I'll meet you in the lobby at 7am, wear something you don't mind getting dirty."

"Yes Sir," Nef said jokingly, then flushed. There nothing joking about the way Alexander's cock immediately strained against his briefs at that statement. And from the way Nef's eyes darted down then up, the way her cheeks flushed further and she shifted her legs closer together, Xander felt even more satisfied knowing she also found him attractive.

Adjusting his jacket, he decided to take a risk. He leaned in and brushed a kiss against each of her cheeks. Her skin was so soft, so smooth, and it was an effort not to linger.

"Nice to meet you, Nef."

"Likewise, Alexander," she responded a bit breathlessly.

"See you tomorrow at 7." waving a hand lazily over his shoulder as he walked away, as though he wasn't painfully hard and desperate to invite her back to his hotel room immediately, Xander congratulated himself on playing it cool. At least until he passed Asim, still with the same lady as before, who gave him a wink and a nod in Nef's direction.

Nef. Joining him tomorrow for the dig. Setting his alarm, he went to mingle with his guests, congratulating everyone on their successful bids and providing commiserations to others.

It was going to be a long night.

Nef welcomed the cool breeze that came in from the open window. It was hot here, more than she was used to. It was late and she lay in bed at last, lips and cheeks pink from where she had scrubbed off her makeup. Clothes for tomorrow's visit to Alexander's dig lay over the back of a chair opposite the bed, taunting her.

Tomorrow. Alexander's dig. Closing her eyes, Nef let her mind replay their earlier meeting. How he had watched her like a hawk while she bid, trying to keep her face calm while her whole body tingled. How he had felt so warm and steady as he walked up behind her at Thuya's mask. The sound of his voice, deep and rumbling in her ear as he congratulated her.

He was absolutely alluring. Nef had had a few lovers in the past, but none who exuded confidence like Alexander did. Just the way he kissed her cheeks had made her want to invite him back to hers for a drink, for more. She wanted to let him help her take off her lipstick, leave smudges on the collar of his shirt and below his belt.

Inviting her to his dig… that was a thing interested men did right? Was this platonic, purely business? But then she remembered her unintentional joke. She had been so worried she had screwed it all up, ruined the image of the professional educated curator she strived so hard to show all the time. But he had definitely liked it. She remembered glancing down in shyness, glimpsing his crotch as he buttoned his suit jacket up. Yeah, he had *definitely* liked it.

So if this invitation wasn't platonic, what was it? And more importantly, what did Nef want? It had been a while since she had ended things with her ex. Plenty of others had been interested since, but Nef wanted commitment this time. Effort. This exhibition was supposed to solidify that for her; if she could put effort and commitment into projects, surely she will attract men who offer the same. But if she wasn't mistaken, if there was a mutual attraction here... a one night stand just wouldn't satisfy her.

Groaning, Nef flopped onto her stomach and buried her head in the pillow. Why couldn't she just enjoy what was happening? She had successfully bid on two items tonight, one of which was a god knows how valuable death mask of an ancient and powerful queen, desired by every collector at the event. A scorching hot man — who she was pretty sure would give her some of the best sex of her life if his bedroom eyes had any say — had invited her to visit his dig, which was not only a long-time dream (and fantasy, if she was honest) but also allowed her to find more items for her exhibition. Maybe... maybe Nef could be a one night stand kind of gal. Maybe she deserved to have a bit of fun, to put herself first. She had needs too.

Her mind drifted back to Alexander. If she was a one night stand girl... he obviously like being in control. Which was a good thing, because Nef didn't. At least not in the bedroom. What would a night with him be like? She was pretty sure it would involve multiple rounds. Maybe even multiple orgasms.

She slowly started stroking her breasts. Long, slow strokes that drifted over her peaked nipples, down her stomach, under the lacy edge of her boy shorts. Lower, until she brushed a finger along her slit, already wet. Pushing a finger in slowly, Nef imagined it was Alexander between her legs. His tongue moving in that fast, strong movement she liked so much. Running her hands through his perfect, soft hair. His beard leaving red marks on her neck and body from where he had kissed and sucked.

And when she was dripping, sick of teasing herself, she grabbed her vibrator from her suitcase and imagined it was Alexander's cock pushing inside her, filling her up, that she was grabbing his strong shoulders as he fucked her against the wall, the windows, the floor.

She came with a small cry, the sound wiped away by the breeze that rushed into her room. Finally exhausted, Nef drifted off to sleep, worries about seeing Alexander tomorrow fading into dreams.

CHAPTER 4

Alexander had been up very, very late. And although that was normal after an event like the auction, for once it hadn't been because he was working, or keeping up another woman. It had been just him and his hand, and thoughts of Nef and those fucking perfect red lips of hers.

Lips which were again painted a deep red, but instead of that tease of a black dress she was wearing fitted khaki trousers, sturdy brown boots, and a loose red collared button up shirt. Practical, light, and sexy. How that blouse closed over those breasts, Xander didn't know and didn't care.

"Good morning," he said gruffly. Dressed similarly in trousers and a tight black t-shirt, he tossed the keys to the jeep to Asim who was waiting at the door of the hotel.

"Thanks again for inviting me," Nef said, falling into step beside him. "I'm excited to see the dig, how long have you been working at this site?"

"We've been here since October 2022," Asim said, jumping into the drivers seat. "Been almost a year now, but we've got a few more sites in mind in Egypt before we head over to Turkey or Israel."

By 'we', Asim meant him and the rest of the dig crew. Xander would be heading back to San Diego to start that new project of his. Visions of a museum in a busy city flashed before his eyes. Xander had had his eye on it for a year or so now, ever since it had started gaining success. There was something masterful about the exhibitions there, but he hadn't yet decided if he wanted to continue the museum or turn the building into a function hall.

Hadn't Nef said she was a curator at a museum in San Diego? He should ask which one. It was probably a small one, considering she came alone to the auction. Most big museums sent multiple representatives, all of whom tried to bid (or in the British Museum's case, 'take ownership of') as many pieces as possible.

Before he could ask though, Nef had swung herself into the passenger seat of the car. Grinning at his surprised face, she shrugged.

"Shotgun. You were too slow."

Letting out a small chuckle, Xander gracefully got into the back seat. Nef seemed...playful today. He wondered if that playfulness extended to other activities.

Down boy, he thought to himself. No need to be an overexcited teenager again. If he wanted Nef to end up in his bed, he would be a man about it. Slow, sure, and not distracted by his own desire.

Nef settled into her seat as Asim started driving. Xander let Asim lead, pointing out the major landmarks and not-so-major landmarks, including his favourite kebab shop in the back alley of a spice market. Dust kicked up as they drove, and at one point they had to dodge a herd of camels, which Nef gleefully took photos of.

"Nef," Xander leant forward so she could hear him over the engine. "Have you travelled much before?"

She turned her head towards him, loose curls brushing his cheek.

"I did a small trip between high school and college with some friends, travelled around Europe right before the pandemic hit. I always planned to come back, but study and work took up more of my time than I expected." Nef sighed. "I did do two years of an exchange program, but this is my first time in Egypt, and my first time travelling properly as an adult." She blushed at that.

Was she embarrassed by her lack of travel experience? Surely not. Exchange was no small thing to discount. Maybe he was projecting, but Xander made a noise of assent anyway. "I get that, I also put off a lot of my travel plans during college. Mostly only travelled between states to meet other collectors."

"What was that like?" Nef sounded genuinely curious, nothing like those other girls who asked him that then immediately babbled on about how cool it must be always on the move for work. He liked that about her, the way she engaged with everything he brought up. He was liking a lot about her. Enough to be honest when he replied.

"It was alright. Moving around got tiring though, and I was sick of being viewed as an amateur. My grandfather was an avid collector, left everything he had to me out of spite to my mother."

Nef wasn't looking at him, but he could feel the question on the tip of her tongue.

"My mother married a man my grandfather didn't approve of. He ended up leaving while she was pregnant with me, proving my grandfather right. I guess I was lucky he liked me."

It came out more truthful and bitter than he had expected. Maybe it was the fact she wasn't looking at him, maybe it was because Asim remained quiet and let them have their moment. But he kept going, eager to tell Nef more about him and his earlier life.

"I started collecting out of a need to prove him wrong, that I deserved to have his inheritance. And out of spite, before I started funding projects and digs and exhibitions, I sent every cent to my mother."

Nef finally turned around properly to face him. They were so close, he could see the flecks of black in her coffee coloured eyes, feel her breath on his lips.

"My father only ever gifted my mother empty beer bottles and bruises."

Xander's heart squeezed tight.

"My aunt is the one who truly raised me. Gave me a job curating for her even though I was barely in my first year of community college. I didn't let her pay me. I only asked that my name be in the credits for each exhibition. That's why we have the funds we do, to buy that death mask, to travel here to find more artifacts."

A truth for a truth, it seemed. Xander wanted to close the distance between them, lick the bitterness out of her mouth, offer her a job that payed more than she could probably imagine not out of pity but because anyone who could outbid David by a million bucks deserved it. By the way Nef was glancing at his lips, it seemed she wouldn't object to the first part of his plan, at least.

But before he could finally taste those cherry lips of hers, Asim pulled into the dig site with a loud series of honks. Whipping apart, Nef and Xander both cleared their throats, sharing a smile in the rearview mirror.

"Lets go habibis!" Asim closed his car door a bit harder than necessary. A good reminder to Xander about where they were, what they were here to do. Subtly adjusting his pants, he quickly escaped the backseat and managed to open Nef's door for her. holding out his hand, he gave an exaggerated flourish.

"My lady? Allow me the pleasure of showing you my kingdom."

Nef laughed, and the stupidity of it all melted away as she took his hand, sparks travelling up his arm. Holding his gaze for a beat too long, she nibbled on her bottom lip. He wanted to do that for her.

"Lead the way, your highness."

The site was incredible. If incredible meant dusty, with a faint stench of old sweat and mummified organs, which to Nef it did. And yes, mummified organs definitely had a distinctive smell.

Xander had introduced her to a few members of his team, all of whom were welcoming if distracted with cataloguing various bits and pieces of shabtis and mosaics. Tents had been set up around shovel test pits, where men and woman in loose white clothing, shielding them from the burning sun, sifted sand and delicately brushed off ceramic sherds.

It was everything and nothing like what she had imagined. And was almost enough to distract her from how close she had come to kissing Xander in the car.

"Xander," he walked slightly ahead of her, leading her to a more permanent tin shed on the outer edge of the site. She gently grabbed his bicep to slow him down, and almost forgot what she wanted to ask when she felt his muscles tense and flex beneath is black t-shirt. Her mouth became very dry.

Licking her lips, she glanced up at him quickly from beneath her lashes. His blue eyes were bright and focused, intense. She licked her lips again, and noticed the way he tracked the vector of her tongue.

"Xander," she said again. When had she become so informal with him? Remembering her question, she pushed through thoughts of running her tongue along *his* lips. "Back there everyone was only looking at sherds and pieces of pottery or ceramics. Where did your bigger pieces like the death mask come from? Surely it wasn't simply dug up from a pit."

Xander let out a low laugh. Nef realised her hand was still on his arm, and quickly stepped back.

"We found a tomb a few miles out from here. Took us a while to get it open, and longer to persuade my superstitious team to actually enter, but we found most of the larger pieces there."

"Makes a lot more sense," she said with a wry grin.

"If you want to see some bigger pieces," his voice dripped with innuendo, making her clench her thighs together. "Then you're going to love what I'm about to show you."

Taking her hand, he tugged her towards the shelter of the shed. Nef felt a thrill as he pulled her along, the roughness of his palms bringing to life fantasies of them running over her body, between her legs. Warmth pooled in her centre. Holding hands — at least in this case — was definitely not platonic.

I could do one night stands, she thought. The small voice in the back of her mind whispered otherwise. But as Xander pulled her into the cool darkness of the storage shed, she ignored it.

CHAPTER 5

Shelves lined every wall, stuffed to the brim with busts, shabtis, urns, and other relics. Everything had a neatly labelled tag, and was numbered in some order Nef didn't fully understand. In the middle of the room, tables and makeshift podiums held similar items and scrolls, designs of what must be the tomb they came from, and maps with various markings.

Nef took it all in with wide eyes. Xander still held her hand, and she was hyper aware of how he watched her, his face a mix of hopefulness and hunger. She stepped further into the room, navigating between the organised clutter with the ease of someone who worked here every day. It reminded her of the museum's basement, full to spilling with art and statues.

"It's incredible," she breathed.

Xander moved closer to her, reached towards her. Eyes fluttering closed, she took a deep breath —

"This piece is one of my favourites." Xander reached behind her, spun her around to face the shelf with a hand on her hip. Every piece of her narrowed to that contact, the warmth spreading out and directly to her aching centre. Forcing herself to concentrate, Nef looked at what Xander was pointing to. A small figurehead of Nefertiti's bust was rendered in gold, small jagged pieces of lapis lazuli studded into the metal. Red paint dusted the eyes, flecked off a bit in some places.

"Beautiful," Nef whispered. Xander pressed in closer, his front against her back, and she held back a shudder. Leaning down, he pressed his lips to her ear.

"I haven't been able to stop thinking about your name." Nef's ears were buzzing from the blood pounding through her.

"At first, I thought Nef might be short for Nefertiti." Every word he uttered made his lips brush the curve of Nef's ear, and she closed her eyes.

"But I don't think a girl as special as you would be that predictable. Am I right?"

At some point, Nef had leaned back against Xander's chest. Her head rested on his shoulder, and his hands were lazily stroking up and down her waist, closer to the sides of her breasts every time. She wanted them higher, wanted them under her shirt, her bra, in her hair and her pants.

"You're right," she murmured. Her voice was embarrassingly breathy. Nef had never heard herself sound like that before.

"I know I'm right," Xander murmured back cockily. "So what's your name, sweetheart?"

Toes curling, Nef sighed as his hands slowly reached higher and higher. Pressing herself further into him, she froze as she felt him against her backside. Long, and hard, and every thought almost left her brain when Xander nipped sharply at her earlobe.

Gasping, she remembered his question. "Nefertari! My full name is Nefertari."

He growled against her neck. "Of course you're named after the most beloved queen."

Nef didn't get a chance to respond. Xander's hands had stopped their gentle exploration of her skin, and she was now flipped around with her back to the opposite shelf. Nefertiti's miniature bust watched on with unseeing eyes as the rough wooden shelf scratched at the exposed skin of her lower back, her red blouse having lifted after Xander's ministrations.

She couldn't tear her eyes from him, his full mouth slightly open, chest heaving against hers. Dangerous territory. She could end it now with a word.

His lips crashed to hers, and all thoughts emptied from her head. His tongue stroked into her mouth, the taste of him causing her to let out a moan loud enough to echo. Encouraged, Xander's hand snaked into her curls, deepening the kiss and setting Nef alight. Tingles erupted all over her skin.

As if he knew, Xander shifted, his other hand moving to cup her brazenly between her legs. A small groan escaped him.

"God, you're already so wet for me."

Nef moaned, rocking her hips softly to try and create friction.

"Not yet, beautiful girl," Xander whispered in her ear. He nibbled at her lobe, leant further down to press an open mouthed kiss to her neck. "When I fuck you, it's not going to be in the middle of a dig site. We're going to be alone, somewhere where I can make you cum without distractions."

Breathlessly, Nef slithered her left hand between them to palm Xander's impressive length.

"What if I want distractions?" She asked. "What if I want you to fuck me where anyone could find us, where if I scream your name loudly enough, someone will hear?"

"Fuck," Xander groaned, head tilting back as he moved closer, the friction between them increasing. Footsteps scuffled from outside the shed, and Nef moved to pull alway.

Clicking his tongue in disproval, Xander tugged Nef by the wrist towards a more sheltered alcove near the back of the room, the artwork around them continuing to observe silently.

As the footsteps started to slow, Xander flipped Nef so her front was towards the new shelf, unable to see what was happening. As he did, Xander's left hand gripped her wrists tightly above her head, and his right dipped below the waistline of her pants.

"Shhh darling," He whispered into her ear. Another kiss was pressed to her neck. "I'm going to make you cum now."

Nef let out a small whimper, undulating as Xander slipped a finger into her centre. As he started pumping his finger slowly, he continued, "Don't make a sound. If you do, I'll stop right now. Understand?"

Nef nodded frantically, writhing on his fingers as Xander added a second.

The footsteps were moving slowly into the shed now, between reliefs and statues at the front. Nef couldn't care less. Every nerve was on fire, her focus narrowed to where Xander's thumb had started to gently flick that sensitive nub at the apex of her thighs. She was so close.

Swallowing a whimper, Nef realised that she had unconsciously spread her legs, and was now unrestrainedly riding Xander's fingers. He moved his hand then, angling his wrist to reach deeper, harder, and Nef shattered into her climax, biting her tongue to keep from moaning.

Panting, she twisted as Xander let her wrists go. Holding her stare, he brought his fingers to his mouth. And sucked them both clean.

❖

Xander didn't know what had taken over him. He paced quickly in front of his hotel room windows, cursing himself soundly. One second he had been showing Nef one of his favourite dig finds, and the next he was making her cum against a shelf while someone was rummaging around the front of the shed.

From the knowing glances Nef had given him over dinner though, she didn't seem to mind. Xander had immediately lost track of the conversation, Nef's sexy little whimpers as she came apart on his fingers taking front and centre.

God, the things he was going to do to her tonight. That is, if he ever got a chance to invite her back to his room.

It was late, and Xander had been ready to follow Nef out of the dining room where his dig crew still sat, when the crazy professor had called him. She had sent through the forms for the transfer of ownership of the museum and respective block of land, but it had gone to his address in San Diego. Now, it would be another week before he would be home to sign them.

Dragging a hand down his face, he slipped his phone back in his pocket. He didn't even know how that professor had gotten his private number. And now he had lost Nef in the maze of the hotel. At least he knew she would be in this hotel, where all the auction guests were staying.

Sighing heavily, Xander stripped off his dig clothes and changed into gym shorts. There were more productive ways to work out his frustrations.

***

The clang of the dropped weights echoed off the marble walls of the hotel's gym. Almost as fancy as the lobby, Xander admired the neatly set out rows of machines, separated from the 82 foot swimming pool across the room by a wall of glass. Sweat dripped slowly down his back, and he heaved in breaths as he pumped his arms and legs harder, faster. The treadmill whirred beneath his feet, the only other sound in the gym as the last trickle of fellow travellers left for the night.

Xander hated running. But he hated not being good at things more. A very healthy coping mechanism that his therapist loved to constantly discuss. Watch finally beeping, he slowed into a warm-down walk, taking a big drink from his water bottle.

There were benefits to exercising, of course, beyond the aesthetics and stamina it provided him. Mostly, it helped Xander think. And tonight he had needed to think.

He wanted Nef. He wanted her more than for just one night, because every time he thought about the shed he thought about how much better it would be when it was his cock rather than his fingers buried inside her. And the thought of doing that multiple times (not in one night) didn't set off the usual alarm bells. Was it because he had actually interacted with her before inviting her back for a night of drinks and sex? Was it because he had seen her humour, her quick wit and honest vulnerability and it matched his own?

He pulled out his phone and switched off his music, set a reminder to call his therapist tomorrow. God bless healthcare workers who put up with his shit.

He did need to be honest with himself though. Yes, he liked Nef's personality, and her body. But he still wasn't sure if going beyond one night was what he really wanted. His collection, his new museum, those were his priorities, always had been. Someone he had just met wouldn't change that, and he'd be stupid to let it.

One night with this woman was safe. It would be satisfying as hell, and Xander definitely wouldn't be left craving more. It would be just like all the other nights, just this time a little more drawn out. One night would have to be enough.

When the gym doors opened and Nef strutted in wearing a dark hoodie that barely covered the tops of her thighs, that thought wobbled.

When she dumped her bag at the side of the pool, and stripped off to her form fitting, red, one-piece swimsuit, that thought started to fade entirely.

And when she turned to grab her hair tie, revealing her soft stomach and a whole lot of cleavage, Xander had to grab hold of that thought like a lifeline.

He was so fucked.

CHAPTER 6

Nef was still recovering from earlier. Her core ached from Xander's ministrations, begged for more, more, more. She could barely look at him through dinner without blushing. Hadn't stopped her though. Xander had kept meeting her sly glances, his gorgeous blue eyes promising more. She had been so eager to leave early but had forced herself to be patient. But when she had finally gotten up from the table, throwing a heated glance at Xander behind her, he hadn't followed.

Stupid, she thought to herself. She had waited for half an hour in the lounge by the lobby, but he hadn't come. Two hours later, and she was hot, horny, and *pissed* — at him, and at herself for thinking maybe he wouldn't be a one-time kinda guy.

Although… a hopeful thought popped up. Xander hadn't finished, and she had felt exactly how much he probably wanted to. Surely he wouldn't make her come then discard her without getting his turn? At the very least, Nef wanted to return the favour. And if he wanted her to return the favour, then maybe this wasn't a one-time kinda thing.

Nef sent off a quick prayer to no-one. She had thought they had had a nice day, a nice date. After Xander had finished with her, they had quickly adjusted their clothes and hair, and managed to start talking softly but exaggeratedly about the pieces on the shelf in front of them. Just in time too, as one of the women from back at the site rounded their corner, placed a reconstructed shabti with a neat label on the shelf next to them, and promptly left, no doubt to tell the other team members about her rumpled boss and new, equally rumpled, friend. Xander and Nef had left the shed in a fit of laughter, spent the rest of the day helping collect sherds into neat piles of similar shapes — kind of like a jigsaw puzzle, which Nef had enjoyed — and ended with whipped ice cream from a Turkish parlour back near the hotel.

It had been the best date she'd had in a while.

Huffing to herself at the memory and the sheer chutzpah of Xander to not have come looking for her tonight, Nef stripped off her favourite hoodie and chucked it by the bag she had dumped by the edge of the hotel pool.

Located on the 16th floor and decorated in marble and sandstone like the lobby, wide floor to ceiling windows showed off the view of the Nile and the bustling city, still alive with the sound of hawkers and car horns. A one-way glass wall blocked off her view of the gym to her right, likely empty at this time of night.

A swim would cool her down, help her think. She snapped on her goggles and dove into the cool depths. As she started a slow lap, Nef let her thoughts about Xander float away with the bubbles. She reached the end of the pool and flipped around, starting another lap. She reached two laps, then three. Nef kept swimming, enjoying the peace that came from moving, nothing but the sounds of her kicking and her blood rushing through her head.

Finally, she slowed at the deep end of the pool. Gasping for breath, she tossed her goggles on top of her hoodie and hauled herself out of the water. Buzzing with endorphins, Nef padded towards the bathrooms at the back of the room, dripping a trail of water behind her. Cursing at the slippery marble floors, she made a mental list for her plans tomorrow.

It was her last full day in Cairo. Having already done the typical sight seeing, she now needed to finalise her auction success with Xander and get the pieces shipped safely to her aunt's museum. Once that was done, she had to pack for her flight the day after.

And then that would be it. Back home, to finish the exhibition and keep ignoring the future of the museum. Nef knew she'd have to find another job soon, but that wasn't something she wanted to think about yet. She also didn't want to think about what leaving would mean for her and Xander, the first man she'd met in years who she actually liked on multiple levels. He was gorgeous, funny, smart, and understood her love of archeology. He was...

He was right in front of her, a small towel wrapped around his waist, dripping water from the showers she had just entered.

They stared at each other in shock before Nef finally broke the silence.

"I thought the gym would be empty this time of night," she blurted out.

"Sorry to disappoint you," Xander joked.

Shaking her head, Nef stepped closer to him. Every part of her craved his warmth, his solidness.

"Not disappointed," she smiled. "Just surprised. If you saw me swimming you could have said hi, you know."

The reproach in her eyes must have been clear, because Xander frowned.

"You looked preoccupied. I didn't want to interrupt. I usually come to the gym to clear my head so I hate being disturbed. I assumed you'd feel the same."

Nef nodded, eyes shifting to the bench behind him. Normally she did feel the same, just not when it came to this man.

Seeming to sense her mood, Xander moved forward and gently grasped her chin, forcing her to meet his gaze again.

"I promise next time I'll say hi."

It was all Nef could do to not lean in and kiss him. Instead, she forced herself to ask him "why didn't you come after me tonight?"

Xander dropped her chin and stepped back, brows lifting. Nef flushed. She had sounded so petulant, so clearly rejected. She was an experienced adult, god damnit. She needed to get a hold of herself.

"I just meant —"

"I meant to come after you," Xander interrupted. Nef stopped talking.

"I had every intention of following you out, but then I got an important call and had to go straight to my room to take it. By the time I was done, I was ready to go straight to find you but I have no idea what room you're in."

Xander smiled ruefully, a slight blush creeping up his cheeks at the admission. Nef wanted to kiss it away.

"I suppose would now be too late to invite you back for a drink?" Xander's voice had turned rough.

Nef cupped his face in her hands, ran a finger over his soft, full lips. Xander's eyes fluttered closed.

"I have some time." Ignoring the thoughts that swirled around her, reminding her that she hated one night stands, that she was leaving in two days, she leant in and kissed him.

❖

Xander had never been so lucky in his life. First to have found Nef, and then to be kissing her again. Nef moaned as he deepened their kiss, tongues dancing, and he reached around her to grasp her wet curls with one hand and her ass with the other. As he did, he realised that he had dropped the towel from around his waist.

Nef whimpered as she shifted her hand to palm his length, finding nothing but warm bare skin. Shuddering under her touch, he pressed open mouthed kisses to her jaw, her neck, the tops of her breasts.

"Take this off," he growled, tugging at the strap of her swimsuit.

Nef obeyed instantly, turning around and flashing him her naked pussy as she pulled the wet garment over her hips and down her legs.

Xander grabbed her waist, tugged her towards the shower cubicle closest to them for more privacy. Before he could ask Nef what she wanted, she had pushed him back against the wall, causing him to bump the tap.

Hot water spilled over them, and Nef let out a low laugh. In the warm glow of the automatic lights, hourglass figure glistening with droplets of water, she looked like a goddess. Large breasts with clear tan lines from her swim suit, topped with rock hard brown nipples. Curls soaked and curling over her shoulders. Her stomach felt warm and soft beneath his hands, and pussy was neatly shaved, a small triangle of trimmed hair forming an arrow to his final destination.

Catching her eyes again, Xander smirked as he saw her dilated pupils, the way she took him in similarly. Nef's hands had been idly stroking his shoulders, his abs, lower.

Nef suddenly dropped to her knees, and Xander's heart stopped.She ran a hand up and down his cock, and he twitched beneath her. She knew what she was doing, and Xander felt a sudden rush of jealousy directed at whomever had taught her. Glancing up at him beneath thick eyelashes, Nef licked her lips.

"I want you to show me how you like it," she breathed. Water continued spraying over them, and Xander could only nod as Nef licked at the tip, then around his length.

Pressing a hot, wet kiss to his head, she slowly sucked on the tip, adding a hand to the base of his shaft and stroking. Tilting his head back against the shower wall, Xander cursed long and loud. Smiling around him, Nef took him deeper, deeper, until he felt the back of her throat.

Xander snapped, the feel of her tongue and throat making him come undone. Fisting her hair like he had imagined from the first time he saw her and those red lips, he started thrusting into her mouth. Pleasure ran up his spine, compounded by Nef's breathless little moans as she continued to stroke what wouldn't fit in her mouth.

God, he was going to come soon.

"Nef, Nef honey I'm close," he panted. Nef moaned, and somehow took him even deeper.

Hips stuttering, Xander groaned. "God honey, you're gonna make me cum so hard."

She kept stroking, sucking, licking, teasing. And when he felt his balls start to tighten, when Nef pulled back and directed his member at her full breasts, he came with a yell, stars sparking behind his eyelids.

Panting, Xander watched as Nef stood up, pressed a kiss to his mouth, and washed herself clean in the spray.

"Enjoyed yourself?" she purred.

"Obviously," he grinned. Every thought in his head urged him to kiss her, take her, make her his. But when he reached out, Nef backed away, opening the stall door and grabbing her towel from her bag, discarded on the bench from earlier.

"It's late. I'll see you in the morning, Xander." With that, Nef took her bag and left.

CHAPTER 7

The phone was on its 6th dial tone when Sophia finally picked up the phone.

"Nef you bitch, you were supposed to call me days ago!" Her friend's voice boomed out of the speaker, and Nef quickly turned the volume down.

"I've been distracted, sorry Soph," Nef cringed. Neglecting her best friend had not been planned, and this was a poor excuse.

"How's Cairo? How was the auction? I'm sure you kicked butt." Animalistic chattering sounded in the background. Although it was currently 1am for Nef, it was 3pm for Soph, which meant she would be at her research lab doing god knows what to some poor mice.

"Is now a good time? I can call later if you're busy!"

"All good babes, now is great! I just finished collecting samples so don't stress. Now tell me what's up. I know you, and you never forget to call then call days later at whatever weird time it is for you at the moment."

The chattering lessened slightly, and Nef smiled. She and Sophia had been thick as thieves since college, when they had met in first year doing the same elective. Glass blowing hadn't been relevant to either of their degrees, and they had trauma bonded through many shattered pieces, burns, and shared love of Reese's Pieces.

Letting out a sigh, Nef got straight into it. "Ok so here's the tea. Basically, I slayed the auction, won the main piece, and have since gotten in-ti-mate-ly associated with the host, who is — excuse my French — like a fucking Greek statue but with personality."

It took a second for it to click, but then Sophia was squealing along with the mice.

"Ok ok ok so first off, CONGRATULATIONS! I told you you'd kick butt. Second, tell me more about this Greek god of yours, holy shit. I thought you hated one night stands though?"

Nef winced, though Soph wouldn't be able to see her. "I do, that's kind of the issue."

Silence in the background. Sophia was always good at listening to Nef's problems, giving her space when needed to get her thoughts sorted.

"So, we got to second base two days ago, then third base last night…" Nef trailed off.

Soph let out a loud whoop, then an apology to someone in the background. "You're gonna have to clarify for me love, who did what to who?"

Groaning, Nef told her everything, fanning herself at the memories.

"It sounds like you want more from this, love. You never have been good at one night only events — and that's not a bad thing!" Sophia quickly clarified. "But if you want more you should tell him. Didn't you say you've kind of had one date-ish? And that he's from San Diego?"

Nef nodded, then remembered it was a call. "Yeah, date *ish*, and he is."

"That doesn't sound like someone not interested in more. Plus, you'll be in the same city!"

"I know, but what if I'm misreading things? What if he does just want to sleep with me then leave?" It hadn't happened to Nef yet, and she wasn't planning on ever allowing herself to get into that situation.

"You'll never know if you don't ask him, love. Relationships have to start somewhere, and communication is essential." Soph would know, having been disgustingly in love with her boyfriend of three years. "And you won't be comfortable doing anything more with this guy — one night or not — unless you tell him what you want."

"I hate it when you're right." Nef grumbled.

"I know," Sophia's self-satisfied smile was evident in her tone. "And I'm always right."

"Go torture your mice, you monster," Nef laughed, tumbling back into her bed. Letting out a slow breath, she wished she had called her friend earlier. She hadn't realised how lonely she had been feeling lately.

"It's for SCIENCE," Soph complained. "Love you Nef, keep me updated. Good luck!"

"Love you, I will." Nef hung up and popped her phone on charge. Drifting off to sleep, she promised herself to talk to Xander tomorrow.

Xander sat at a dining table in the hotel's breakfast room, a plate of pastries untouched in front of him. His coffee was cold, and the papers on the table seemed to be laughing in his face.

Last night had been… confusing. It had also been one of the best blowjobs of his life, at least until Nef had left without any explanation. Usually, he was the one to leave quickly, once his promise of a single night had been fulfilled. The women he'd been with before hadn't seemed to mind. Had he done something to upset Nef?

Giving in to his hunger, he dug into a cherry danish. Ignoring the coffee — iced coffee just wasn't natural — he looked around the room again.

"Why so nervous, Alexander?" Asim slumped into the chair opposite him. Helping himself to the cold coffee, he ignored Xander's half hearted protest and waved to someone behind him.

Declan and Erik dropped into the remaining chairs at the table, matching smirks on their faces. The Irish and Swedish PhD students had become fast friends with Xander and Asim, and were using the dig as one of many sites supporting their thesis. He would have loved to know what they were researching, but Declan refused to show anything he wrote and he doubted Erik had even started.

"Has he admitted anything yet?" Declan drawled in a thick accent.

"He was just about to when you lot showed up and interrupted," Asim nudged Declan in the ribs with an elbow.

Leaning forward to avoid the scuffle, Erik chimed in. "I thought you had a one night stand policy? Why are you nervous if you have already..." he made a rude hand gesture, his turn to get elbowed by the others.

"Actually..." Xander cleared his throat and shifted in his seat.

The guys stared at him, realisation slowly dawning.

"She *rejected* you? Pay up, fellas!"

"No!" Xander said indignantly. "Wait, you bet on this?"

Declan slowly sat back down, sheepishly handing some notes back to Asim and Eric.

"I mean, not specifically, but, I mean... well, yeah. Sorry mate." They all at least looked guilty.

"Its fine guys," Xander relented. "Anyway, we've done… things. But it's none of your business."

The guys all started clamouring at that.

"Ok ok calm down! Animals, honestly." The young men sat back, waiting. So Xander filled them in bits and pieces — not everything, he wasn't one to kiss and tell, but enough so they got the gist of things.

"You're telling me she's the best you've ever had, and you haven't even slept together yet?" Erik's eyes were wide. "Why do you get all the luck?"

"Because he looks like that," Asim jokingly gestured to Xander's chest.

"Keep your voice down!" Xander hissed. "Anyway, I don't know if I upset her or something. I was planning to ask her back to my room, but she…"

"Left?" Erik chimed in with a sympathetic grin.

Xander groaned and gripped his hair in a fist. "I just don't know what she wants!"

Declan whistled, and Xander shot him a glare.

"Maybe she doesn't want just one night. Thought of that, Xander?"

Xander blinked. Declan had a point. But he hadn't had a proper relationship in years. Thinking about it though… it didn't repulse him like usual.

As though reading his thoughts, Asim lightly punched him on the shoulder.

"Technically, you've already had more than one night with her. What's stopping you now? You're already ahead!"

Xander put his head in his hands. These idiots were his best friends, but it had taken years to be able to talk about anything deeper than work with them.

All around the same age (Erik the youngest at 29 and Asim the oldest at 31), they had travelled almost five countries together, slept in the same awful, waterlogged, tents together, and discovered some of the finest collections of ancient art and history together. If not for them, he would have fallen apart when his mother had died, and might have even given up collecting entirely. Deciding to finally pursue additional projects still within the realm of archeology had in part been thanks to their ideas.

"I don't know," Xander responded quietly. "I just don't think Nef would be ok with my kind of relationship... I can't promise her what she deserves. We'd be in the same city, but I'm starting this new project. You know how important this is to me. More than Nef."

The guys looked at him sympathetically. Deep down, Xander knew what he had said was true. He would always prioritise his projects, and Nef did seem like the kind of woman who'd want more. More calls, more visits, more everything until it became too much for him.

Asim clapped him on the shoulder, bringing him back to earth.

"Ok firstly, are you even sure she wouldn't want to try things your way? Have you asked her?"

Xander stared at his friend, feeling stupid. He hadn't asked her. Had it really been so long since he'd had more than a single night with someone that he had forgotten how to actually date properly?

Nodding to himself, Asim continued. "Secondly, you've already been on a date, technically. We all saw you at the dig. Are you sure one night stands are what *you* want anymore?"

Xander stayed silent, the realising that maybe... maybe he *did* want more. Maybe he was willing to try.

"Ah, I thought so," Asim sat back smugly, reading whatever was written on his face. "Anyway," he nudged the others to start leaving. "Here's your chance to ask."

CHAPTER 8

Nef entered the room in a whirlwind, curls flying behind her. Glancing around, she spotted Xander at a breakfast table in the far corner by the windows. Asim and two others were leaving, flashing her wide smiles as they headed back towards the buffet line. Smiling shyly back, she waved and picked her way towards the table.

As specified in the auction invitation, if successful with your bid, the finalisation of the transaction would take place throughout today at specified time slots. Nef had been allocated 9am, and while usually punctual, had overslept after her phone call with Soph and was now five minutes late.

"I'm so sorry I'm late," Nef gathered the skirts of her loose white dress under her as she sat down in front of Xander.

"That's ok," he responded stiffly.

For a few seconds, they stared at each other. Mentally shaking herself, she opened her mouth to speak.

"Lets get straight to it," Xander beat her to it, neatly shuffling the papers in front of him with a tight smile.

"Xander…" she stopped him with a hand on his wrist. Xander froze, staring at where she gently ran her thumb over his hand.

Nef took a deep breath. "I need to explain about last night."

"You don't have to." Xander's voice was a deep rumble, and she wanted it against her chest, skin to skin.

"I do," she insisted. "I didn't mean to leave so suddenly. I'm sorry if I made you feel weird because of that. I want to put all my cards on the table."

Nef held up her other hand, stopping whatever Xander had been about to say. Continuing to slowly swipe her thumb back and forth, she kept talking.

"I really like you, Xander. I haven't been in a relationship in a while, and I'm not a one night stand kind of girl." She smiled grimly as Xander moved to take his hand back.

"I figured you would be," she said sadly. "I've really enjoyed getting to know you, and I don't want to complicate things especially because I'm leaving tomorrow morning. That being said, I wanted to ask what your thoughts are. If you're open to it, I know we're both going back to San Diego, and I'd love to know where you'd like us to stand. I'll respect whatever your decision is, but I can't continue like we have been if you don't want more than just one night. I'm sorry."

Xander had been fiddling with his cufflinks as she spoke. Now, he leaned forward and took her hand, which she had left on the table.

"I appreciate you talking to me, Nef. You don't have to apologise for sticking to what you're comfortable with." he said.

Oh god. Here it comes, the 'lets leave it here' conversation that while inevitable, had Nef holding her breath hoping otherwise.

"I haven't been in a relationship in a long time either. And I'll be honest, it's usually because archeology will always come first for me, never the girl."

Nef's heart sank. Here came the kicker.

"But I really like you too. I can't promise a relationship, I can't promise anything really, especially because I'm about to get started on a new project and I don't know what that will mean for me yet."

She was nodding, a bit shocked. He liked her? But he didn't want a relationship? What was happening?

"What I can promise though, is that I can be a perfect gentleman when warranted." Xander fixed her with a look hot enough to melt her panties. "You warrant perfect, and a gentleman. So if you're ok with seeing how things go, and keeping things… casual, can we start with a date? Dinner tonight, I'll pick you up at seven?"

Biting her lip, Nef broke into a wide grin. "A date sounds perfect."

Xander was good at a lot of things. Some things he knew from experience, and others from people telling him. But standing at the door of Nef's hotel room (which he finally got, along with her phone number after they finished signing all the forms for the art pieces), holding a bouquet of red roses, Xander did not feel like he was good enough for this woman.

She had apologised to him for leaving unexpectedly. She had explained herself articulately, and put herself first. She didn't accept any one night stand crap, and she let him know it. And she liked him — although that part he had gathered from the night before.

Xander really should have been dating more beforehand, because it wasn't until Nef had swept in, looking hot as hell in a white linen dress, lush curls, and those deep red lips, that he had realised that confident self aware women were apparently a turn on for him. Like a rock-hard, had to stay sitting until the end of his second appointment, level of turn on.

He had liked her telling him what she needed. He wanted to know, needed to know, and needed to do and be those things for her. Xander had been ready to book her in for every available piece of free time he had until she left, but he also knew that that definitely wasn't casual, and they both had agreed to start slow and see what happened.

So here he was, dressed in black pants and a fitted white button down with the sleeves rolled at the forearms, hair combed beard trimmed and holding a big bouquet of fresh roses, ready to take things slow.

Come on, Xander, he thought, rocking back on his heels. You've done this before. You know how these things go. Man up and knock already! Reaching up, he rapped loudly on the door. It sounded much more confident than he felt.

The door swung open to reveal Nef, somehow looking more breathtaking than the auction. Her dress was bright red and figure hugging, stopping just below the knees. Her halter neckline had a horizontal cut out, showing the barest hint of full cleavage. With kohl swept eyes, deep red lips, and matching black shoes and nail polish, Xander almost fell to his knees.

This woman had been made to be worshipped.

"You look incredible," Xander leant in to kiss Nef's cheek.

A faint blush crept up her ears, drawing his attention to a small cluster of freckles under the corner of her left eye.

"You do too," she said shyly.

"These are for you," Xander held out the roses with a flourish. "Would you like me to put them in water for you?"

Nef was fully blushing now, a wide smile on her face. Nodding, she opened the door wider to let him in.

"They're beautiful, thank you so much" she admired the fresh petals, running a finger across the delicate veins. Xander held back a shudder, remembering that finger elsewhere, moving in a similar way only a day ago.

"I love how punctual you are," she continued, as she found a small vase by the back of the desk. "Have you always been like that, or is tonight just special?"

Her smile was teasing, but Xander sensed a deeper purpose to the question.

"Do you always ask questions like this, or are you just trying to get to know me?" He teased back.

"Guilty," Nef laughed. "You can't blame me though, isn't that the purpose of a date?"

Humming a noise of assent, Xander helped fill the vase with water and placed the flowers in. He had kept one back in his room so he would know when they died and could send her more. He suddenly realised that he had done that despite her plans to leave tomorrow morning, subconsciously already planning to ask her on another date, to stay longer.

"I want to know everything about you," he said in a low voice.

"Ask away, Xander. I'm an open book." Nef's eyes flashed with mischief, and she sauntered over to take his hand. Unable to stop himself from following the sway of her hips, he reached out with his other hand to grab her waist, partly to feel her solidness, her warmth, and partly to ground himself before he did something stupid.

"I can ask anything?"

Laughing, she wrapped a finger around a strand of hair that had fallen over his eyes. Tugging lightly in a way that sent a thrill straight to his cock, she leant in until her breath skimmed his lips.

"Anything you want, honey." The endearment almost undid him, more than hearing his name in her mouth.

"I want to know..."

Nef stopped him with a finger over his lips.

"Save it for dinner, Xander," she winked. "I have a feeling some questions are best asked and answered over food, rather than in a hotel room."

Entwining her hand with his, she snatched her bag and pulled him towards the doorway. Mouth finally catching up to his head, Xander grinned and closed the door behind them. Leaning down to whisper in her ear, he caught her shiver as he got the final say.

"Some questions will require a hotel room, but I'll save those for dessert."

CHAPTER 9

By the time they reached the restaurant, Nef's mouth was watering, and not just from hunger. The drive had been quiet. Xander had driven them, one hand on the wheel and one hand on Nef's knee, lightly stroking with his thumb sending tingles straight to her core. The silence was comfortable though, occasionally punctuated with Xander pointing out a landmark that he had visited, or worked in, or that sold the best baba ganoush. It seemed he had visited Cairo often, which she admitted when asked what his favourite city was. He had a preference for Egyptology over anything Greek or Roman, and also had a small collection of Persian relics that he kept back at home, hence his penchant for constantly visiting the Middle East.

"What do you do with all your pieces?" Nef laughed with incredulity. "How can you possibly store them all?"

Xander had shot her a grin. "I can't," he admitted. "But I have some loose plans."

"If you ever feel like you have to much, don't be afraid to donate some to a good cause." Nef said slyly.

"I take it you have a cause in mind?"

"Of course — me." she replied simply with a smile.

Laughing, Xander had squeezed her knee.

"I'll keep you in mind, Nef. You get first dibs."

Xander had driven her to Pier88, an Italian restaurant situated on the river Nile bedecked in glittering chandeliers, warm candles, and dark moody lighting. Couples dressed in even fancier clothes than themselves dotted the tables throughout, but a waiter had led the pair to a separate table on the outside balcony, away from the low bass music and sounds of the kitchen.

A champagne bottle was already chilling in a bucket beside them, and Xander held her seat out for her. Blushing at his chivalry, he pushed her seat into place before rounding the table opposite her.

Nef raised an eyebrow at him. He raised one back.

"You have to tell me how you got a reservation at a place like this in 24 hours."

Running a hand through his hair, Xander grinned sheepishly. "You got me — I'm friends with the owners. My grandfather used to bring me here all the time."

"You've mentioned him before. He got you into collecting, right?"

Xander nodded, moving to fiddle with his top button. Already undone, it revealed a sliver of his bare chest, tanned and taut beneath the fitted shirt. Taking a sip of water to offset her suddenly dry mouth, Nef asked another question that had been on her mind.

"What made you stay in the business?"

"I love everything about it." Xander met her eyes, a soft smile on his face. He had stopped fiddling with his button. "At first, I just loved the pieces, loved seeing how they all fit together to make a story. But the more I collected the more I loved the rest of it — the auctions, meeting crazy personalities who liked the same things I did, going to the dig sites and actually seeing where these masterpieces came from."

Nodding, Nef leaned in intently. She knew what it was like to love everything about a job.

"I eventually got into funding my own dig sites through a mix of loans and running my own auctions. Like you said, where was I supposed to store this stuff? I figured letting museums buy it, to have it on display so people like me could enjoy it was a worthy thing to do. And then I could go find more objects."

"That's incredible. It must be very fulfilling, to be doing what you love every day. And getting to travel for it too." Nef said.

Xander nodded, reaching for the champagne. "It is. What about you though? How did you get into curating?"

Taking a sip from the glass he proffered her, she pondered how to respond. "It's complicated."

He exaggeratedly shuffled forward in his chair, propped his head on his hands.

Chuckling, Nef continued. "I had always worked at museums. Not curating, yet, but I knew I would have loved to if given the chance. I worked at the ticket desk then as a tour guide, but I originally went to college to major in law. It wasn't until two years in that I realised I was ignoring my essays in favour of planning exhibitions, so I switched majors. Did a post-graduate masters in art history and curatorship in Sydney, then came back to work as a curator. The exhibition your pieces will be in will be my first official one I directed on my own."

She glowed with pride at that. As much as she was dreading leaving tomorrow, leaving the certainty she felt when she was next to this man, she couldn't wait to finally start putting her drafts into action.

"Incredible," Xander echoed her earlier words. He shook his head slowly. "I have so much I want to ask and feel like not enough time."

Nef's smile fell. Right. Just tonight. And see how things go. Pasting her smile back on, she said brightly,

"Better ask me now then."

He reached for her hand across the table. Before he could speak, a waiter came over to take their order, but Xander waved him away without taking his eyes off Nef's.

"You're worth making more time for."

Nef felt a flutter low in her stomach. The urge to kiss him was rising with each second, and she gripped the edge of her seat with white knuckles, trying not to leap across the table. Slow. They were taking things slow. As if pulling the thought from her head, Xander kept speaking.

"I know this is sudden, and we said we'd take it slow and see how things go. But what do you think about me paying to extend your flight so you can come on another date with me?"

Nef's heart stopped. The shock must have been evident on her face, because Xander started to pull back, apologising.

"No no, don't apologise! That would be, I mean, I'd love to!"

Xander's face split into a smile, tugging on her heart.

"But I can't make you pay for my flight, I'll call and change it later tonight."

"Nef," Xander squeezed her hand gently. "I think you're forgetting your place."

Her brows drew together in confusion. Her what now?

"*I'm* taking *you* on a date." He emphasised. "Tonight, and in two days from now, to a charity ball run by my friend in Dubai. And I will pay. Not just because I can, and I honestly don't care whether you can or can't, but because I want to. Let me treat you, Nef. Please."

Flustered and thrilled, Nef nodded slowly, not looking away from the intensity of his gaze. "Thank you Xander." She smiled.

"No, thank *you*." Xander let go of her hand, and picked up the menu. "Let's order?"

Smiling, Nef picked up her menu. One date in, and boy was she in deep.

Three hours later and dessert was still in front of them, though Xander was focusing more and more on what he'd rather be eating.

Tonight was amazing. It was still amazing, almost four hours in, from the second Nef had opened her door. Why had he been against doing this, again?

So far, he had discovered that Nef was 27 (only two years younger than him), had a wicked sense of humour, and shared his love for reality TV and disdain for procrastinating. It was almost scary how similar they were, how passionate they felt about the same topics. It had kept them talking for hours, even while many other restaurant patrons had come and gone.

The woman in question was luminescent in the warm glow of the candle at their table, talking animatedly and visibly more relaxed after a glass of champagne. Not normally one to drink (and, he had found out, neither was she) he also felt a bit more relaxed, and was enjoying the success of his romantic planning. Admittedly, he had asked Asim for some tips. Some had been useful (hence the champagne) and some had been ridiculously inappropriate.

Nef slowed to a stop, her rant about California's dismal museum funding coming to a close. She was adorable when she got all worked up about something, Xander had discovered. He wanted to get her worked up in multiple different ways.

Sensing the change in mood, Nef's soft smile turned sharper, more sultry. She finished off her basbousa with a flourish and unnecessarily suggestive flick of her tongue.

Setting down his own fork, Xander waited a few beats before standing up, trying to distract himself with thoughts of literally anything but Nef. Catching the eye of the nearby waiter, he motioned for the check.

A few moments later he had paid, and was walking back to the car with his arm draped over Nef's shoulder. Even while wearing heels, she only came up to his chin, which he found endearing. Leaning down, he pressed his nose to her hair, breathing in her citrus and vanilla perfume.

"Tonight was fantastic," he murmured in her ear.

Nef smile up at him, and leaned further into his chest. He wanted every inch of her pressed in a similar position, with less clothes between them.

"I can't wait to do this again," she murmured back, hope shining behind her eyes.

Something uncomfortable shifted in his stomach at that look. He wanted to promise her a million more nights like this one, and that was the problem — he wasn't sure yet if he could.

CHAPTER 10

Xander held his breath as they reached Nef's hotel room, subconsciously tapping his fingers against his thigh in anticipation and anxiety. He had been so eager to finally reach this point, but that was when he had been sure it would only be for one night. Now, it was something completely different, and he wasn't sure how he felt about it.

Did he want this to happen? God, yes. Did he think it would end well? He had no fucking clue, and that scared him. Xander wasn't worried about how he would take things — after all, it had only been a few days — but what if this kept going? If it did work out? What if it kept going and crashed and burned when he prioritised his new museum, and he had to live with breaking Nef's heart? Did worrying about breaking Nef's heart mean he was already emotionally invested? It had been so long for him he wasn't sure he could remember what that felt like.

This was what his therapist called 'catastrophising'.

Suddenly, they were in front of Nef's door. She turned, propping a hip against the door and fixing him with what he had come to know as her signature smile.

"Thanks again for tonight, Xander," she said, running a hand down his arm. She stood there expectantly, and Xander wasn't one to deny a beautiful woman what she wanted.

"It was my pleasure," he said smoothly. Stepping forward, he caressed her waist, cupping her jaw with his other hand when her eyes fluttered closed. Leaning in, he pressed the barest hint of a kiss to her lips.

Nef let out a small sound that had his cock rushing to attention. Staying still, Xander let Nef take the lead, deepening their kiss and sliding her hands up his chest and around his neck.

More. Xander wanted, no, needed, more. Pressing Nef against her door, he slid his hand into her curls, tilting her head back so he could kiss her deeper. Her moans were getting him drunker than wine, and Xander couldn't help a groan of his own when she tugged him closer by his belt.

Hands were everywhere, and he realised he had started grinding against her like a teenager. The thought that he should stop, pause, maybe move out of the public corridor disappeared like smoke when Nef popped open two more of his shirt buttons and slid her hands underneath the soft fabric, lightly grazing his nipples with her nails.

Xander sucked in a sharp breath.

"Lets move this inside," he ground out.

Nef responded with an enthusiastic noise against his lips, and Xander reluctantly released her leg, which he had hitched up around his hip in an effort to get closer to her.

Breathless, a dress strap pulled out of place, and with red lipstick smudged against her cheek, Nef let them into her room but didn't turn on the lights. Catching sight of himself in the large mirrored closet on the wall right of the bed, Xander looked just as bad — shirt half open, red lipstick marks all over his lower face and neck. He wanted them lower, wanted to put his own marks on Nef's lush curves.

"We haven't talked about sex yet," Xander growled.

Nef dumped her bag on the desk and made a show of bending over to take off her shoes. Crotch uncomfortably tight, Xander mimicked her and placed his shoes by the door.

"Considering the last few days, I was under the impression you know that I'm very much ok with it." Nef winked.

"Oh I know, sweetheart." Xander enjoyed the blush that had started creeping up Nef's face. "I meant how you like it."

"Like — what I enjoy in bed?" Nef had moved back in front of him, and there was something disarmingly cute about a glammed-up Nef in bare feet, now barely up to his collarbones.

"Yes, Nef," Xander rumbled. He placed both hands on her hips, gently moving her backwards towards the bed. Through the windows on the left, the Nile sparkled with reflections of the city skyline.

"Tell me what you like in bed."

The order rang through her, and Nef shivered. Xander towered over her, perfectly in control, silhouetted like a Greek statue against the light coming in the window.

"I like it when you tell me what to do," she whispered.

Xander grinned like a wolf. "Anything else?"

He had started fiddling with the hem of her dress, lifting it higher and higher in a slow teasing motion. Emboldened, Nef admitted what she had barely told past lovers.

"I like not having control. I like…" Nef broke off into a moan. Xander had lifted her dress over her hips, and was lightly trailing his fingers over her underwear.

"I want to know what you want, Nef. Stop denying me."

Xander pushed aside the lacy material and slowly slid a finger into her centre.

"Fuck," Nef swore. "I want it rough. I want to experiment. Please Xander, keep going just like that…"

Two fingers now, filling her up just like in the shed. Nef was gripping his broad shoulders for dear life, the delicious feeling of Xander's firm pumping making her eyes roll back.

"Anything for you, sweetheart." He pressed a kiss to her collarbone, then withdrew his fingers entirely.

Nef's cry of protest quickly died in her throat as Xander started to strip. Removing his shirt, then his pants, Nef couldn't decide where to look first. His chest was defined and tanned, leading to lines of abs she wanted to lick. A deep v led into his navy briefs, where an impressively large member strained against the material.

Despite her previous experience, Nef had a second of panic about whether Xander would fit inside her.

"Strip."

The commanding tone had her snapping to attention, peeling away the dress and her matching lingerie. Keeping eye contact, Nef tossed her clothes into a small pile before sliding back onto the bed, spreading her legs slightly and watching Xander's predatory gaze move straight to her pussy.

"You never told me what *you* like in bed," Nef's voice was huskier than she had heard before.

Finally removing his underwear, Nef's mouth watered at the sight of his cock. Fuck, he was big. And thick. And while she had managed to take him in her mouth earlier, she wasn't sure if she would be able to take him inside her. Wetness leaked between her thighs, and her breasts tightened with her rising need.

Xander crawled on top of her, stealing her breath with a kiss. She could feel him brushing against her stomach, and couldn't resist reaching between them to stroke him gently, loving the silk and steel feeling of him in her hand.

Letting out a small moan, Xander clenched his eyes shut.

"I like control." He nipped at her earlobe. "Someday, I'm going to help you experiment. Show you exactly what I like"

He gripped her wrists, pinned them above her head with one hand. The other hand had gone back to pumping inside her, his thumb lazily stroking her clit. She needed more pressure... maybe shifting her hips would help?

Xander quickly removed his fingers again, pinned her down with a hand over her soft stomach. Unable to move, Nef breathed heavily, more turned on than ever.

"Someday," Xander continued, "I'm going to tie you up in my favourite red ropes, and I'm going to show you what no control means."

Nef let out a whimper. God, she wanted that. She didn't know she would until he said it.

"But tonight…" Xander kissed her again, tongues clashing as they each fought for dominance. Breaking the kiss, Xander released her wrists, slid onto his knees the floor, and dragged Nef by the ankles to the edge of the bed.

She let out a yelp of surprise, but then Xander was spreading her legs, stroking the sensitive insides of her thighs.

"Tonight, I'm going to worship you."

And with that, he went to work. Gripping his hair with one hand and his hand with the other, Nef lost track of time as Xander licked and kissed in ways that made her see stars.

He made sure to avoid where she needed him most though, instead sucking and nibbling the sensitive skin around her clit. When he added a finger, Nef's legs started shaking. When he finally made his way to the apex of her thighs and sucked, Nef's back bowed off the bed as she came with a scream.

Slowly coming back to her body, Nef breathed hard and waited for the feeling to return to her legs. A satisfied male face appeared above her, and Xander wiped at his mouth with a grin.

"I hope you know I'm not done with you yet."

Nef grinned back. "I certainly hope not."

"I have a condom in my wallet," he looked around for his pants, lost in the chaos of earlier. Nef just nodded.

She got STI tested yearly, and had an IUD, but she and Xander hadn't even talked about exclusivity yet. Better to be safe than sorry.

She watched as Xander deftly rolled it on, and he crawled on top of her again. Hovering between her legs, Nef closed her eyes as Xander lined up the head of his cock with her pussy, anticipation gushing through her blood.

"Please, Xander," she whispered.

"Open your eyes," he ordered quietly. Nef did, and found him watching her closely, observing every shift in her face. "I want to see you reaction when I enter you."

Xander slowly started to push inside, his gasp mixing with her own. With small thrusts of his hips, Nef felt waves of pleasure wash over her. One last shift, and Xander was seated fully inside her.

Foreheads pressed together, Nef was panting. She felt so stretched, so perfectly full. Then he started to move.

"Oh god, oh god," Nef cried.

Her nails were scratching at his back, her legs locked around his hips. Xander was panting harshly against her neck, muscles bunching in his arms he held himself above her.

Without withdrawing, Xander shifted, lifting Nef's legs over his shoulders and reaching a place deep inside her that made her scream.

"Fuck yes, Nef," Xander moaned. "I want you to cum with my name on your lips."

He thrust harder, and Nef's vision went white.

"God, Xander, harder, *please*." Nef was begging now, so close to that blissful edge. Happy to oblige, Xander picked up his pace, slamming into Nef. Letting out a growl, he slipped a hand between them and stroked her clit lightly.

"Xander!" Nef was shaking with the force of her second orgasm. Shuddering, Xander buried his head in Nef's neck with a shout, thrusts coming to a stuttering finish.

He collapsed on top of her, and Nef stroked the soft strands of his hair as they both caught their breath.

"Wow," she said softly with a giggle.

Chuckling, Xander looked up long enough to kiss her cheek gently.

"Wow," he agreed.

CHAPTER 11

The next day, guests had mostly left and all the auction items had finally been packaged and sent on their way. After a lengthy call with his airline, Xander had managed to get an extra seat next to him to fly to Dubai with Nef, and had alerted his friend Danilo about his plus one. Now, he stood in the hotel's gardens, having just finished up a call with that professor again to confirm that the forms were signed correctly.

All of his tasks had taken significantly longer than usual, and his frustration must have shown because Asim had intervened after lunch.

"Oi, the one who looks like a lovesick puppy!"

Xander's glare had Asim backtracking quickly.

"I mean, my friend! My very good, very old friend." Asim reached out a hand to grab Xander's shoulder, then apparently thought better of it.

Good. Xander only wanted to be touched by one person right now, and she was busy.

He hadn't been able to stop thinking about her since he left her room this morning. He had stayed the night, a surprise to even himself. Nef must have some kind of mind reading superpower, because the second he woke up and thought about leaving before she woke, she had rolled over onto his chest, her leg entwined with his and her head nestled in the crook of his neck. They had fit together like a puzzle piece, and before he knew it, Xander had fallen back to sleep.

So that's how he had ended up running late to his first meeting, and to every other errand of the day. Being late wasn't the issue though. Not seeing Nef was.

By the time they had woken up, halfway through breakfast, Nef had several missed calls from her aunt. Nef had promptly kissed him, kicked him out of bed, and promised she would meet him for dinner before they caught their next flight.

Asim was still talking.

"Sorry Asim," Xander said tiredly. "I missed all of that."

Asim grinned. "I know, Alexander. I'm just teasing. I'm not here to torment you —"

"Are you sure?" Xander grumbled good-naturedly.

"I will pretend I never heard that. So, what I was saying, is that I'm here to stage an intervention."

Xander raised an eyebrow. Asim's interventions were... interesting. They were always a surprise, always a bad idea, but (mostly) done with good intentions. Like during their first dig together in Eilat, when Asim had taken it upon himself to help Xander get over his fear of sharks. Turns out 'acclimatising' him with a marathon of Jaws was not, in fact, the best way to try do that. Half shuddering, half chuckling at the memory (less terrifying over time), he relented.

"I guess there's nothing I can do but go along with it?"

"Look at that, the handsome millionaire is smart too! Man I hate people who have everything."

"And you have almost everything - apparently I inherited the brains." Elbowing Asim with a laugh, Xander followed him back inside. "What crazy intervention do you have this time?"

Wagging his eyebrows, Asim looked far too smug for his own good.

"See for yourself," he gestured widely towards the doors of the lobby.

Nef watched Asim's grand gestures with a small smile. Today had been hectic. First, she had to kick poor Xander out so she could call her aunt — they were close, but NOT close enough to call while she had a man in her bed.

After catching up with Aunty Tiye and making some tweaks to her exhibition blueprint, Nef had enjoyed brunch at the local markets up the street, practicing (and butchering) her Arabic. It was there that she had been ambushed politely by Asim. Now, she watched as he put their hastily made plan into action.

"I promise — stop Xander, trust me — I promise I packed your suitcase in the 'correct way'," Asim's gestures were getting more outrageous by the second.

Xander murmured something she couldn't hear.

"Yes, yes, of course I thought this through! It's all organised, you have no choice."

Holding back a laugh, Nef observed the two friends as Xander rolled his eyes exasperatedly. It was clear how close they were. She felt a pang in her chest, and quickly shot off a text to Sophia:

I MISS YOU.

MISS YOU TOO! Came the fast response. *HOW'S YOUR TALENTED HUNK?*

Nef bit her lip to hide her smile at the series of winky faces that accompanied the text. While packing earlier, she had sent a very detailed voice message to her best friend. It seemed that the only details Sophia had absorbed were those about Xander's... abilities. Not that she could blame her. Nef was also very interested in said abilities.

Before she could respond, Xander was walking towards her, smiling cockily. Blushing at the unmasked hunger in his eyes, she shifted her feet nervously. She hadn't really said bye properly this morning, and this was the first time she was seeing him after the date. Did she hug him? Kiss him? Shake his hand? They technically weren't even exclusive yet.

Xander solved her internal panic pretty quickly. He strolled straight up to her, cupped her jaw in a hand, and kissed her. Nef melted into him, wrapping her hands around his neck and pressing herself to his body. Soothing strokes of his hands ran down her back, and Nef gasped as Xander gently nipped her bottom lip. They broke apart slowly, and Nef knew she was smiling dopily.

"Hey," she whispered. His eyes were such a gorgeous blue. She debated repainting her bedroom wall at home to match.

"Hey yourself," he whispered back. "You ready to go?"

Nodding, Nef grabbed his hand and turned to get her bags.

"Bags are sorted!" Asim dove for the bags, Nef's suitcase looking like it was ready to split down the middle. Xander shook his head amusedly.

Smile wide enough to split her cheeks, Nef settled into the car that had been waiting outside, Xander climbing in next to her. Of all the 'interventions' Asim had regaled her about throughout their meeting at the market, this had to be the best one: an early flight to Dubai, and all of Xander's work covered for 48 hours.

***

Nef loved the fact that an hour into their three and a half hour flight, Xander had passed out on her shoulder. Earlier, he had looked edible as usual in his fitted shirt (maroon this time) and black slacks. Most noticeable though had been the matching bags under his eyes. She knew he had slept through the night with her, but maybe that wasn't normal for him? Xander had told her just how much he was working, but Nef hadn't realised just how much of a toll it seemed to take.

Reaching out slowly, she tentatively stroked his hair behind his ears. Running a finger tip lightly down his forehead, Nef traced the straight slope of his nose, the sharp angle of his jaw, the roughness of his beard.

Memories surfaced of last night, when they had been wrapped around each other, trading secrets in the dark. One particular moment had stayed with her.

Nef had been on the verge of falling asleep, Xander's chest pressed against her back, one arm under her head and the other wrapped around her chest, lightly stroking her stomach, the tops of her breasts. Unaware that she was still awake, Xander had spoken softly.

"I'm scared I'm going to ruin you."

Sitting next to him now, his breath tangling in her hair, Nef frowned as she replayed his words. What had he meant? Ruin her how?

Breathing stuttering for a second, Xander blinked awake and sat up groggily. When he saw Nef, a slow grin spread across his face, eyes lighting up.

"Back in a sec, sweetheart" he murmured, pressing a kiss to her forehead.

Nodding idly, Nef opened her texts with Sophia. Soph's last text stared at her from its little green bubble. Typing quickly, Nef sent off her response just as Xander slid back into his seat, holding out a takeaway cup of coffee.

I THINK HE'S GOING TO RUIN ME.

CHAPTER 12

Nef was still deciding if she wanted to kill or kiss Asim when Xander walked into the room behind her, carrying her suitcase like it was nothing. Vividly remembering the feeling of his arms pinning hers over her head, she realised it probably was nothing to him.

Images of Xander at the gym flashed through her mind: Xander's legs bunching as he grabbed his weights, abs rippling, sweat glistening on his shirtless chest...

"I'd say I want to kill Asim, but I'll confess I don't really have a problem with this unless you do."

Xander's voice was nonchalant as he flopped down onto the large bed taking up the majority of the room. Large bed, *singular*.

"I feel like Asim is trying to tell us something," Nef laughed.

Hands on her hips, she looked around at their suite. Asim had done pretty well, she had to admit to herself. Artful blue and white patterns decorated the wall to the right of the door, and the king size bed was pressed against it, facing a sprawling view of Dubai from the 51st floor. A shiny black wardrobe was built into the same wall the bed was against, and a small tv and armchair stood opposite it.

It was a room fit for a couple. Nibbling her lip, she tried to sort through her thoughts. After a lengthy text exchange with Sophia, they had come to the conclusion that she was well and truly falling fast for Xander. He was everything she had imagined in a partner: funny, gorgeous, smart, similar interests and values. As cliche as it was, it just felt *right*.

But Sophia had also been right. While no other guy had made Nef feel this safe so quickly, her feelings weren't unusual. Nef knew she had a tendency to get emotionally attached quickly after sleeping with someone (hence her no one night stand rule). And while this technically wasn't a one night stand, they still hadn't talked about what they were.

Just ask him! Nef yelled silently at herself. You always tell yourself communication is key. Why aren't you asking him!?

The small voice in the back of her mind made unfortunate sense. Whatever this was at the moment, she didn't want this to end, and asking might end this. She was a coward.

Taking a deep breath, Nef made a decision: baby steps. This was technically a second date. A very extended, very extravagant, very *public* second date. But if she waited until they both went back to San Diego in a few days, maybe Xander would feel similarly to her by then, and they could at the very least be exclusive.

Ignoring the voice that kept whispering exactly how thoroughly exclusive she wanted to be, she marched over the plush carpet and set her carry on bag down in the corner next to the wardrobe, before flopping next to Xander on the bed.

"This doesn't bother you, does it?" she frowned slightly.

"Why would it bother me?" Xander shifted onto his elbow to look at her.

"I don't know… the one bed might just be… a lot. Is this too fast? Too… relationship-y?"

Xander reached out a finger, smoothing the crease that had appeared between Nef's brows.

"I'm in a beautiful city with a beautiful woman, who — if I haven't already been abundantly clear — I am ridiculously attracted to. And before you come for me about whether I'm just here for your tits —"

Nef laughed and poked him in the ribs.

"Ow! Let me finish, woman! Anyway, as I was saying, as spectacular as your tits are — which they are, by the way — I am even more attracted to your personality, despite your completely horrendous love of making me try new foods."

"Makhasy is a traditional Egyptian dish, thank you very much! You can't have travelled there as often as you have without trying it!"

The fact that he had called her beautiful made something stick in her throat. Her ex had always saved those compliments like an umbrella for a rainy day, attempting to cheer her up when she felt bad. This felt different though. It felt genuine.

Nef blinked up at Xander, almost nose to nose. Somehow, they had ended up on their knees, his hands on her waist and hers on his chest. Idly, she stroked her hands up and down his torso, over his broad shoulders and biceps.

"Any other dangerous habits of yours I should be aware of, sweetheart?" Xander's cocky grin sent thrills through her stomach.

Eyeing the time on the bedside table clock, Nef reluctantly decided that she didn't have enough time to show him exactly what she wanted to make a habit of doing with him.

"Only that I need at least an hour to get ready for special events." Nef smiled sweetly, letting that sink in for a second.

In a flash, she jumped off the bed, grabbed a bag from her carry on, and ducked through the second door in the back corner. Closing the bathroom door with a flourish, she called out one last time.

"Shower's mine! I'll be ready by 4pm."

Xander's amused groan followed her into the water.

Xander adjusted his tie in the bathroom mirror before checking the time. True to her word, Nef had been out of the bathroom at 4pm on the dot. The sight of her wrapped in a fluffy white towel, curls dripping down her back, had his cock standing at attention immediately.

Unfortunately, Nef had breezed past him, heading straight for her suitcase.

"Your turn, handsome," she had winked.

Xander had dutifully headed into the bathroom, and had been closing the door behind him when he was rewarded with a flash of Nef's lush curves as she dropped her towel.

If Nef had wanted him to pleasure himself in the shower, she had gotten her wish. Not that he would tell her that, Xander thought to himself.

Finally able to zip up his suit pants without straining the zipper, Xander fixed up his hair and checked his watch again. It was now almost 5pm, and a car would be waiting for them in a few minutes, ready to transport the pair to the event space. The location would be kept secret until the last minute, due to Danilo's penchant for mystery. Secretly, Xander loved the intrigue around his friend's events, but this time he was overcome with more nerves than excitement. The last time a 'plus one' had joined him at an event... well, it wasn't something he cared to remember at the moment. Or ever.

"Fuck me," Xander gripped the doorframe for support as he spotted Nef by the window.

It was hard to remember it had barely been a week. He wanted to fall to his knees in front of her, run his hands up that dress and — And he was hard again. He swore softly. So much for that shower.

Turning towards him, Nef's face lit up in a smile. The night's theme was 'Under The Stars', and Xander could have sworn Nef was literally glowing.

Her dress was a floor length, deep royal purple, studded with tiny crystals that danced in the light. The neckline cupped the tops of her breasts in a heart shape, and Xander wanted to peel away the short gossamer sleeves that skimmed her shoulders to confirm his fantasy that she wore nothing underneath.

"Nefertari," Xander ground out. He was still gripping the bathroom door. "You look like a damn queen."

"Alexander," Nef bit her lip, painted a deep wine red this time. "You look... incredible."

Xander tugged self consciously at the lapel of his plum coloured suit, looking down with a smile. The dress code was formal, with a request that the main colour be purple for Danilo's charity of choice. This year, Danilo had chosen The Starlight Foundation, with all ball ticket profits going towards sick Australian children in hospitals.

The hem of Nef's dress appeared in his view. Cupping his face with her hands, she drew his eyes to hers.

"I mean it, Xander. You look…" she gave him a long slow glance that heated his blood. "You look edible."

Nef's voice was huskier, and Xander slowly released the doorframe, reaching for her hip. Pulling her closer, Xander ran his nose along her jaw, pressed a kiss to the slope of her neck. Her perfume enveloped him. He wanted to bathe in it.

Nef's hands had pressed under his blazer, and were slowly making their way to his belt.

"Xander…" she moaned softly as he nipped at the skin where her neck met her shoulder, licked the small hurt away. Reaching for the hem of her dress, Xander started to pull it up her body.

His phone rang.

Cursing soundly, Xander checked the caller ID. The car was out front, and they were going to be late. Grumbling, Xander lightly kissed the corner of Nef's mouth, avoiding smudging her lipstick.

"We'll continue this later. Shall we?" Xander whispered.

Stepping back with a sigh, Nef grabbed his hand.

"We shall."

CHAPTER 13

Nef really was a damn queen, and Xander wanted to be her king. Every moment spent with her seemed to make him remember why a relationship was worth having. He had emailed his therapist earlier, to make sure he wasn't crazy for feeling this way. The good news: not crazy. Apparently, this was a "healthy relationship" and had the potential to "heal his past trauma". He had paid $200 to be told that.

Pushing aside his disdain for the financial issues of the American health system, Xander instead turned his attention to the woman beside him, holding his arm tightly as they stepped into a massive artificial domed tent. A pop up garden had been set up around it, offering privacy to guests who were already getting handsy behind the potted plants. Nef smirked knowingly at him as they passed.

Inside the tent, fairy lights glittered from where they crisscrossed the expanse of ceiling. A mildly famous musician was serenading a crowd on a central dance floor, and tables and chairs dotted the outskirts, flecked by black-clad waiters holding platters of exotic dishes. The dome was washed in purple; tablecloths, drapes, balloon arches, and over 200 guests were washed in every shade imaginable.

Just inside the door, flanked by security guards, a table had been set up with representatives from the charity. Talking animatedly in a lavender three piece suit, a bespectacled man with silvering hair was surrounded by a group of guests.

"Danilo!"

"Alexander! Thank you for coming." Danilo enveloped Xander in an embrace. Spreading his arms wide, Xander's friend turned to take in Nef.

"The mysterious guest Xander told me about! A pleasure, a pleasure," The Filipino took the hand Nef had reached out, kissing her hand with a flourish.

"Oh, gosh," Nef blushed and glanced at Xander in surprise. He grinned at her. Danilo had always been extravagant, and no matter how many times he'd warn people, the effect was the same every time.

"Danilo, this is Nefertari. Nef, this is Danilo, an old friend."

"It's nice to meet you," Nef said. She grabbed his hand again, and Xander felt a thrill at the possessiveness of it.

"It's nice to meet *you*! Xander hasn't brought a proper guest in years, not since —"

"Not for a very long time, Danilo," Xander cut in with a forced laugh. He really should have talked to Danilo beforehand. This was technically only his and Nef's second date, and he did *not* feel like hashing up his last relationship yet. Especially not when the last few days seemed to be going really well.

"How is *your* plus one, though?" Xander continued.

Danilo launched into a monologue about his wife. The man had been smitten for years, and even now, over two decades later, he still took every chance to boast about how wonderful she was. Xander was only half listening, however, distracted by Nef's effortless conversation skills as she was introduced to more of Danilo's friends.

She fit in perfectly here, he thought. Elegant, well spoken. Much more than he could say for the last time. Shoving the humiliation and shame from his mind, he took Nef's arm again.

"Danilo, I want to introduce Nef to some others. We'll speak more later, as usual?" his friend nodded distractedly as more friends came to swarm him.

Walking deeper into the growing crowd, Nef pressed in closer to him.

"What did you mean, as usual?" She asked curiously.

"Remember how I told you that Danilo has been running a charity ball annually for the last several years?"

Nef nodded, dodging a stumbling guest. He frowned at the show of inebriation, pulling Nef tighter and out of the way of being trampled.

"You ok?" Once certain the path was clear, he continued. "We've been friends for a while through work — he was a major source for sending people to my auctions. I've made it a tradition of donating a large sum to his charity of choice each year."

"That's amazing, Xander."

"I have the money. It should go where it's needed."

Nef stroked a thumb down his wrist, and Xander held back a shiver. This woman. She could unravel him with a touch.

"Not everyone thinks like you do. I used to host free tours of the museum for underprivileged kids," Nef said as they reached a table in the back. "I always wanted to donate or volunteer with charity programs, but college and work took up all my time, and any spare money I made I…"

Her breath hitched, and Xander scooted his chair closer, taking her hands in his.

"You can tell me anything, Nef." He squeezed her hands.

Nef swiped quickly under her eyes, and Xander felt a surge of protectiveness. Nothing should be making Nef cry. He wanted to hold her, comfort her however he could.

"My mom was pretty hurt when my dad left us. Physically, as well as mentally. We were ok for a bit, but for those last few years before graduation, any money I made went to keeping up her life support."

God. He remembered what it had been like when his grandfather had died. Xander may have been the favourite, but he had despised his grandfather for what he had put his mother through. Seeing him on life support those last few days had been brutal, but he couldn't imagine what Nef would have gone through.

"I think you're the strongest person I've ever met." Xander tilted her chin up, meeting her glistening eyes.

She gave him a watery smile.

"Sorry for the waterworks," she mumbled. "This charity... I volunteered in some Australian hospitals when on exchange. It brings back a lot of memories."

"You should have told me," Xander was dismayed. "I never want to put you in a situation that might hurt you."

Nef kissed his cheek gently. "I knew what I was getting into. Besides, I like meeting your friends, spending time with you."

Xander leant in and kissed her softly. "I'm glad you're here with me."

"Me, too."

❖

"I'm just going to quickly meet with Danilo for the donation!" Xander shouted to Nef over the music. They were sweaty and crowded on the dance floor, and Nef was having the time of her life. No man had ever made her feel so seen, so special as Xander had tonight.

Every guest they met, he introduced Nef first with a wide smile. He hadn't judged her when she almost started bawling about her mom. Half an hour ago, he had asked her to dance, and had held her close, swaying to the music.

Held securely against his solid chest, Xander's hands slowly running over her back, her ass, her shoulders, Nef had been getting wetter and wetter and was nearly ready to beg him to take her back to the hotel. Xander had known it, too, and had likely been about to offer when his watch had beeped.

"Will you be ok on your own for a bit?" Xander yelled again.

Voice already a bit hoarse from scream-singing to the music, Nef nodded emphatically.

"Wait for me by our table!" Xander waited for Nef to nod again before disappearing into the crowd.

On her own, Nef continued to sway with the guests. She was fully sober, but the energy of everyone around her combined with the darkened lights and loud music gave her a dizzying, out of body feeling.

Time to sit down, she thought to herself. Pushing through the crowd, Nef froze as she spotted someone horrifically familiar.

No. No no no no no.

Not him.

Not here.

Ducking back into the safety of the dance floor, she kept track of him as she looked for the bathrooms. Reaching the safety of shadowed corner, she pressed her back to the cool solid side of the tent and pulled her phone from her clutch.

Be sensible about this, she breathed deeply. It's not likely to be him. First things first: she texted Sophia 3 peach emojis, their emergency code when referring to Mr Asshole. Not an idiot, Nef also sent a text to Xander:

I THINK MY EX IS HERE. AM TRYING TO AVOID. SO SORRY TO DO THIS TO YOU ON OUR DATE!! I'M NEAR THE BATHROOMS BUT WILL GET BACK TO OUR TABLE ASAP.

There. Now if anything happened, even though she knew she was being paranoid, at least there was textual evidence. Her phone chimed; Soph had responded.

NEED ME TO CALL 911?

I'M OK. ALSO I DON'T THINK THAT'S THE NUMBER IN DUBAI.

Putting her phone away, Nef glanced back at the guests. She couldn't see him anymore. Maybe he was just a lookalike. A very accurate, unfortunate, lookalike.

Deciding to brave finding Xander and her table, Nef ducked out of the shadows in a power walk, heels clicking on the faux-concrete floor as the music stopped between songs. In her haste, she crashed into someone.

"So sorry!" Nef gasped. A hand grasped her arm tightly.

"Nef! I was just looking for you!"

The tall, pale-eyed man staring down at her made her blood freeze then curl. Not a look alike after all.

CHAPTER 14

She debated if throwing up on him would make him leave her alone.

Stay calm stay calm stay calm. Clamping her mouth shut, she took deep breaths through her nose, trying not to let Gabriel see how affected she was by him.

"It's great to see you, Nef." Gabriel had grabbed her other arm now, and was sliding his hands over her biceps. She felt like he was smearing grease all over her.

"Unfortunately," Nef gasped out, "I can't say the same for you. What are you doing here."

Gabriel somehow moved even closer, a blond curl falling over an eye.

"I heard you're planning your first exhibition. When I couldn't find my invite in the mail, I knew you had made a mistake, so I asked around a bit to find you. Heard you had won yourself a pretty little statue at some fancy auction."

Nef wrenched herself out of his grip. "I stand by our last conversation, Gabriel. You can go fuck yourself. I'm leaving."

Before she could step around him and the monstrosity of a suit he was wearing, Gabriel's hand shot out and punched her in the stomach.

Reeling, Nef bent over double. Vomit threatened to crawl its way up her throat, and tears blinded her eyes. Blinking her vision clear as the rush of blood faded from her ears, she heard Gabriel talking loudly.

"Just a bit tipsy, thanks for checking folks! I'll take her to the garden for some fresh air."

A small crowd dispersed from around them, purple-clad men and women throwing her alternating sympathetic and disgusted looks over their shoulders.

"You —" she gasped out, standing back to her full height.

"You," Gabriel interjected, wrapping an arm around her and forcefully steering her towards the doors at the back of the tent, "Are not feeling well. Let's go sit down and get some air, yeah?"

Nef stumbled out of his grip and onto a bench tucked behind potted palm trees and rose bushes. The sickly floral scent nearly made her gag again, and she sat forward, putting her head between her knees. Gabriel had punched her. She couldn't wrap her head around it.

"What the fuck do you want from me, Gabriel?"

"Are you here with anyone?" He sat down next to her, too close for comfort.

"What?" Nef looked at him sharply. It was the wrong thing to say.

Gabriel grabbed her chin, hard. "Are. You. Here. With someone."

Raising her head defiantly, she grinned savagely. "I am. And I was just about to meet up with him before you barged in."

Gabriel tutted and shoved her head away. Her neck cracked at the force, and she winced, holding a hand to her chin. Fortunately, she didn't think it would bruise.

"I always knew you were a whore, Nef."

She made a harsh sound, something between a growl and a hiss. Gabriel hadn't always gotten on her nerves. Once, she had loved him. But that had been two years ago, and now even his name was enough to bring up feelings of unadulterated loathing and nausea.

"I wouldn't mind being a whore" she said sweetly through clenched teeth, "if it meant you paid me for all those lousy times I had to fake it with you!"

Standing up, she rounded on him with her bag raised, ready to slap some sense into him.

"Whoa, sweetheart, you're not in any position to do this right now." Gabriel grabbed her bag with lightning reflexes, the hem of his untucked dress shirt — more blue than purple — flapping in the sudden breeze. He stood up, towering over her.

Nef knew Gabriel. Knew he was a prick, but this violent side of him was one she had never seen before. While it made her even more grateful to have ended things when she did, having him here, now, dwarfing her, made her nervous. She knew what could happen to women like her.

"I came to ask you for a favour, sweetheart." Nef bristled, but stayed silent. The sooner Gabriel spoke, she could pretend to think about this 'favour', then run.

Gabriel continued, reaching up to brush her cheek with his hand. Nef flinched, and he scowled. Slapped her face hard enough to sting. Shame washed over Nef. She hated just standing here, but the alternative would be worse.

"About that statue. I bet you've got quite a big budget, huh? And don't feed me bullshit about you spending it all. You've always been so stingy. Anyway, that statue is worth quite a lot, according to those media articles I saw about it."

Nef's blood was freezing over. He couldn't be asking what she thought he was. She knew he had a gambling problem — had discovered it too late — but surely he didn't have the audacity to come to *her*. Not after what he had done.

"Anyway, sweetheart, I need some cash. I know it's been a while, but you know what it's like, living in the big city. And you've always been so good to me. I just need a couple grand."

Her blood was heating now, red fading into her vision. Trembling, she dropped her clutch, hands turning to fists.

"Just a couple grand, Nef." Gabriel's voice turned whiny this time. He stepped forward, taking her hands in his, pressing them to his chest and trapping her in place. "Only a couple grand. Like the last time."

Like last time. The words clanged through her, and Nef snapped.

The donation had gone smoothly as usual, and Xander had been waving goodbye to Danilo and his wife, Maria, when he saw Nef emerge from the bathrooms near the back of the tent.

A smile broke across his face. She had been the best part of this evening. He hadn't properly enjoyed an event like this in years. He couldn't wait to take her home, ravish her. He wondered what she thought about being fucked against the windows... Reaching for his phone, he went to text her that he was on his way.

I THINK MY EX IS HERE. AM TRYING TO AVOID. SO SORRY TO DO THIS TO YOU ON OUR DATE!! I'M NEAR THE BATHROOMS BUT WILL GET BACK TO OUR TABLE ASAP.

The message lit up on his screen, and the smile dropped from his face. Emotions flooded him. Nef had an ex? That didn't surprise him, she was incredible. Anyone would want her. But her ex was *here*? Who?

That earlier surge of protectiveness was back, stronger this time. A sense of possessiveness flooded through him, and although he knew Nef was her own person, he couldn't help the anger he felt thinking about someone being here who might think they had a claim on his woman.

His woman. His to protect, to cherish, to support. She was avoiding an ex. Xander knew what that was like. He needed to be with her, even just to help her feel less alone.

Pushing through the busy dance floor, Xander caught glimpses of Nef throwing nervous glances around the room. She suddenly ducked out of the shadowed corner, and Xander saw her crash into someone in her haste. The stranger was now blocking his view of her. Was Nef ok?

A popular song started playing, and more people rushed onto the dance floor. Jostling through the sea of purple, Xander finally reached where Nef was. Or had been. She, and the stranger, had disappeared. Xander started sweating. Something didn't feel right. First Nef's texts, now she had disappeared. He knew this could just be paranoia, but he'd rather be safe, rather have Nef be safe, than otherwise.

Shoving down thoughts of what could be happening right now, Xander spun around, frantically searching for Nef in that sparkling dress of hers. Surely that and her vibrant curls would make her easy to spot.

A flash of light caught his eye, and Xander saw Nef — accompanied by that stranger — heading towards the back doors. It was a man, and he had his arm around her.

Stomach suddenly queasy, Xander stood and watched as the tall blond man led her into the gardens. Guests parted around him, and he wasn't sure how long he stood staring before a snatch of conversation caught his attention.

"That poor girl, a bit of a disgrace letting herself get that tipsy..." An older man with greying hair was talking to a woman with equally grey hair, pointing in Nef's direction.

"Good thing she had that nice young man to help her," she was saying.

Snapping to attention, Xander took a deep breath. No jumping to conclusions, he told himself. Maybe that couple were referring to someone else. Maybe it was Nef, and she had needed help. The thought didn't sit right with him, though. His gut was telling him something was off, and it had a tendency to be right.

Making a decision, he pushed through a cluster of people and stormed towards the back doors. Sick or in danger, Nef was here on a date with *him*, not some blond douche in a stained tux. If anyone should be helping Nef do anything, it was him.

Throwing open the doors with more force than he intended, Xander heard Nef's voice coming to his left. Rounding the bushes, he came to a stop jerkily.

Nef was standing almost nose to nose with the man. One of his hands was resting on top of hers, which were pressed against his chest. The other hand was moving, slipping to caress the small of her back over the soft material of her dress. Xander felt like he had been sucker punched. He opened his mouth to ask what the *fuck* was going on, but the stranger suddenly let out a high pitched wail.

Nef had moved like lightning. Ripping her hands away, she had brought her knee up so hard between the stranger's legs, Xander winced as well. Nef didn't stop there. She grabbed the man by the back of his neck and shoved his head downwards, and a sickening crunch sounded as his nose met her knee.

Xander could only watch in pure shock as Nef kicked the man in the balls once more, a sense of satisfaction running through him as the man collapsed to the floor, sobbing. Xander ran a hand through his hair, letting out a shocked laugh. He had known something felt wrong, had practically come running to Nef's aid, and here his girl was, protecting herself with ease, proving again how incredible she was.

"Xander!" Nef gasped. "I, I, I'm so sorry, I —"

Pulling himself from shock, Xander ran the last few steps to Nef and enveloped her in a tight embrace.

"Are you ok? Did he hurt you? I saw your text, and then you disappeared. Tell me you're ok. I'll kill him if he lay a hand on you."

He felt Nef exhale against him, shuddering sobs starting to wrack her body. If this asshole had hurt her, he didn't know what he would do.

"Let's get you somewhere safe," Xander murmured into her hair.

Nodding, Nef stayed glued to his side as he got out his phone. Sending a quick text to Danilo, then to Asim, his next contact picked up on the second ring. He may not be able to save Nef from the pain she was currently feeling, but he sure as hell could make sure she never felt it again.

CHAPTER 15

It was late when they got back to their hotel room, but at least Nef was smiling now. They had come straight from the police station, where Nef had given a statement. Upon directions from Xander's lawyer, she had reported the man — Gabriel — for harassment, stalking, assault, and battery.

Xander had also given his lawyer Nef's contact details for any further issues closer to the hearing, not that Nef had to be there. Although, from the smug satisfaction on her face when she saw him in the holding cell, and what he had seen earlier, Xander thought Nef might actually want to be at that hearing. He certainly understood why she had studied law initially.

"Finally," he shrugged off his shoes and blazer before falling back onto the bed with a dramatic sigh, pleased when he saw Nef's smile widen. "You going to come join me?"

Nef hesitated, fiddling with a crystal on her dress sleeve.

"Tell me what's wrong honey. Is it about earlier? You don't owe me an explanation."

There was no way Xander would push Nef to tell him anything. Flashes of his last relationship ran through his head, the pain in his chest bleeding between his own and what he felt on Nef's behalf. He just wanted to hold her, make her feel safe.

Still not looking at him, Nef brushed her curls behind her ears. Her hair stayed put for a second, before the weight of it all flopped back to frame her face.

"I'm just..." she started.

Xander sat up, giving her his full attention. He had found out the basics during the statement; he had refused to leave Nef's side. He knew whatever Nef was about to say would be different, though.

"I'm just so *angry*." Nef scowled. She was cute when she was angry. So not the point right now, but still. "I feel so *stupid*. I did *everything* to cut him out of my life, and the asshole managed to find me *half a world away*."

Nef's voice was rising now. "He had the fucking audacity to ask me for money. Ha! The one time he ever asked. And when he said... he said..." she trailed off, a look of exhausted sadness entering her eyes.

Xander reached out for her, and she crawled onto his lap, straddling him. Head in the crook of his neck, she breathed in deeply while he stroked her back. Having her here felt scarily natural. He wanted to do this every time she felt like this.

"He said he just needed a couple grand. "Just like last time". Asshole," she whispered.

"Can I ask what happened last time? You don't have to tell me anything you're not comfortable with." Xander added hastily. He kept stroking her hair, soaking in her warmth.

"It's ok," Nef leaned back and wiped at her eyes, clearing a tiny smudge of mascara. "I had been saving all my spare money for years, keeping it as cash stuffed in a jar under my bed. Every month or so, I'd deposit it at the bank, in an account that was used to fund my mom's life support."

Xander felt cold then hot as he started to connect the dots. He almost didn't want Nef to keep talking.

"I was supposed to deposit the money that day. But my work called me cause they needed another receptionist, so I called Gabriel and asked him to do it for me. It was the first time I had ever asked, and he was so eager to help. He had been so supportive, for three years at that point, he was practically family. I was so sure he was it for me." Nef sniffled.

"He promised it had all gone smoothly, so the next time I needed to make the deposit and he offered, I said yes again. I was picking up extra shifts, I thought I was even making enough to maybe save to... to travel."

Xander's heart was nearly breaking. His mom may have been treated like shit by her father and husband, but he felt eternally grateful that she had been there for him until the end. Everything he had done had been for her.

Nef kept going with her story, a small bitter laugh tumbling out of her.

"Three months later, I got a call from the hospital asking if I was coming that afternoon, to be there when they switched off my mom's life support. I didn't know what to say. My aunt and I literally ran there, and I kept calling Gabriel asking him to come quickly.

The doctor explained that they hadn't received the money for months, and that it was policy to switch off life support after three months no payment. Said it was too expensive for the hospital and that the money was needed for other equipment.

So I watched my mom die, and caught Gabe in my room when I got home literally red handed with the empty jar I used to use. I broke up with him on the spot."

"I'm so sorry Nef. That never should have happened." Xander was still stroking her back, long smooth sweeps that had her sinking deeper into his arms.

After a few minutes of just holding each other, she kissed his jaw lightly. "Thank you Xander. For listening, and for not being scared off by earlier. And for everything else."

Xander smiled, his chest warm. It was a privilege being told Nef's secrets, and he told her so.

"I will say though," he began, "I was ready to kill him myself when I saw him touch your back."

"My back?" Nef laughed, cupping his jaw.

"Yes, Nef," Xander growled. "That was our date he interrupted. I don't like it when other men touch my date."

"Oh?" Nef was smiling slyly now, and he knew that meant trouble. "So you'd hate it if another man touched me? What if he just touched my arm? What about my hair?"

Xander went still at the thought of some other man running his hands through Nef's curls. Nef noticed, raised an eyebrow at him.

"Someone's jealous," she purred. "What if I like having other men look at me?"

"You don't, though." Xander pointed out stiffly.

"True. But I like seeing you all wound up and serious. It's sexy."

Xander shifted, starting to grow hard at the change in Nef's tone. He remembered that she was straddling him, and he started to harden further. Nef seemed to remember her position at the same time he did, because she started shifting her hips in small circles, the friction forcing Xander to hold grit his teeth.

Nef seemed to forget what her place was. It seemed he had to remind her. Xander grabbed her hips and stood up suddenly, ignoring her surprised gasp and carrying her around to the edge of the bed. He placed her down and kneeled above her, admiring the way her curls splayed across the covers.

"The things I want to do to you…" he breathed heavily.

Nef was panting equally heavily. "Do it, Xander," she said. "I want all of it."

God, he wanted to do all of it. Surging forward, he captured her lips in a kiss, stroking his tongue into her mouth, nibbling her bottom lip in that way that made her moan.

"I have ropes in my suitcase," he said as they broke apart. Staring into her eyes, he felt gratitude and something else as he saw the trust in them.

"If you use them on me, you never use them on any other woman again." Nef's smile was teasing but her tone was hard.

"I'd rather burn them than have them touch anyone else," Xander promised.

"Then get the ropes."

"I want you naked. Now." Xander was at his suitcase in a flash. Finding the ropes in their bag under a bunch of underwear, Xander relieved himself of his own clothes, a button almost popping off his shirt in his haste.

Nef was naked and waiting on the bed, a position he was sure would never fade from his memory as long as he lived. Pulling out the ropes, spurred on by her excited grin, he got to work.

CHAPTER 16

Xander was staring at her, admiring his handiwork. Kneeling on the plush carpet, Nef revelled in the feeling of the red ropes snaking over her body, holding her legs apart and arms behind her back. Excitement fizzled her blood, and her chest heaved as she breathed deeply in an attempt to be patient. She hadn't realised just how much she loved bondage. She wanted to do everything, try everything. All of it with Xander, this man she hadn't known for long but already trusted with her life. Literally, after the events of the evening.

Walking in front of her, Xander caressed a curl from her cheek and leaned down to whisper in her ear.

"Do you understand why I'm doing this?"

"Yes Sir," Nef breathed. She didn't plan to say it, but it felt right, and she saw Xander's cock twitch as he came to a stop in front of her.

"Tell me."

"Because you need to mark your property?"

Xander fisted a handful of Nef's curls, twisted her head surprisingly gently closer towards him. It took everything in her to not lean forward and take his impressive length in her mouth.

"Partly. But mostly to remind you that you're mine, and that no one else gets to even look at you."

The memory of Gabriel trapping her hands to his chest, stroking her lower back, punching her in the stomach, tumbled through her. Nef let them come. He couldn't hurt her now. Not when she had this strong, sweet, sexy man at her side.

Xander tugged her hair again, his cock brushing against her lips.

"Suck." He ordered. "You know the way I like it."

Eagerly, Nef kissed the tip of his member before swallowing him whole, rewarded by Xander's low moan.

"God yes sweetheart, take your man's cock just like that."

Whimpering, Nef shifted forward, ropes tickling her sides as she tried her best to take Xander deep into the back of her throat. With her hands tied behind her, she couldn't pleasure him like usual but she was determined to please him as best she could. The next minute she spent sucking, kissing, and licking up and down his member, eliciting as many groans as possible.

Wrenching herself off Xander's cock with a gasp, she begged him, "please cum down my throat Sir."

Xander cocked an eyebrow and slipped his sex back into her mouth, thrusting gently. Moving back off him, Nef pleaded again.

"Please Sir," she begged, "Please cum on me, inside me. Mark me as yours. I need to be marked as yours."

Thank god for growing up with Cosmopolitan — her dirty talk seemed to be working. Nef surged forward and took him back into her mouth, deeper than before, eliciting another groan from Xander.

"Get on the bed," he growled. Grabbing her by the ropes, Xander practically dragged Nef onto the pillows, freeing her hands quickly before re-tying them to the legs of the bed.

"If you move, I stop," was his only warning before he knelt before her at the end of the bed, parted her sex with two fingers, and started licking like his life depended on it.

"Oh god, oh god, Xander please don't stop!" Nef didn't care they were in a hotel room. Didn't care if the walls were thin. She just wanted more, all of it, all of him.

"If you speak again, I'll stop." Xander briefly looked up before adding two fingers to his ministrations. The sight of Xander fingering her between her legs while she was tied up with ropes like a birthday present made Nef moan. She was so wet, aching for him to fill her up properly, two fingers not nearly enough.

Continuing to pump at a steady pace, Xander murmured, "you look so good impaled on my fingers. I can't wait to see you impaled on my cock."

A small sigh escaped Nef. With a few more minutes, Xander could probably make her crack, and she wouldn't be able to stay still.

"Cum for me darling," he ordered, lowering his mouth to her pussy again. He continued to lap at the bundle of nerves while twisting his fingers until he hit a spot that made her legs quake. With a muffled scream, Nef came for him, legs rising unbidden to wrap him in a vice.

"Oh god, Xander," she breathed.

But Xander wasn't done yet. Gripping her legs tight, he yanked her closer to the edge of the bed and continued to suck on her clit, alternating between long, slow licks and quick circling motions with his tongue. Within minutes, Nef was screaming and coming beneath him again.

As Nef recovered, Xander slowly undid the ropes, allowing her arms to rest gently on the pillows. Kissing his way back down her chest, he payed special attention to her sensitive nipples, making her squirm and moan.

Suddenly, he slammed into her wet and warm pussy, thrusting steadily. Nef clawed at his back and arms. Nothing but their breaths sounded between them.

Leaning up, Nef captured Xander's mouth with hers, a long slow kiss at odds with his increased pace.

As suddenly as he had entered her, Xander was gone, the lack of being filled causing Nef to whine.

"Turn over," he demanded harshly. "Have you ever been spanked before, sweetheart?"

Nef shook her head. "I've definitely wanted to be, though."

"Then turn over. Don't make me repeat myself."

Flipping immediately to her stomach, Nef obediently offered her pussy to him again, raising her bottom slightly off the bed.

Smack!

Xander's arm came down twice more, leaving a red handprint on both butt cheeks. Gasping, Nef arched her back further, a silent offering for him to take what was his. Xander grasped her hips tightly and slammed home again, setting an unrelenting pace.

Nef was in heaven. The feel of him as he slid in and out, the solidness of his chest against her back, the sounds he made as he groaned into her ear with each thrust. She was so close already. She never wanted to stop.

"Touch yourself for me love," Xander breathed raggedly into her ear. "I want you to come all over my cock until I fill you up."

Not one to resist an order, Nef slipped a hand below her waist. Moaning, Xander's pace slowly became more erratic.

"I'm so close love. Don't stop touching yourself. You come first or none of us come."

Supporting himself on one arm, he licked the arch of her spine and placed the other hand gently around her neck.

"Oh my god I'm coming! Fuck, Xander, I'm coming for you!"

Nef felt her muscles tense and relax in sequence, and Xander let out a yell as he came deep inside her, filling her up. Collapsing next to her, he rubbed her back as they both gained their breath.

"So," Xander panted. "I take it you also like the idea that no one gets to touch you but me?"

"Yes Sir," Nef winked.

CHAPTER 17

Waking up with a dead arm and a mouthful of Nef's curls, Xander smoothly detangled himself from where they had been spooning so he could order them both room service. Speaking softly, he requested that Nef's pancakes would have extra maple syrup, and quickly changed his order of poached eggs to scrambled. That sorted, he climbed back into bed gingerly, trying not to wake up Nef. She stirred awake anyway, turning over and reaching for him with eyes still closed.

Her beauty crashed into him again. Clothed, naked, whatever form she took seemed to leave him simultaneously breathless and breathing heavily, needing to touch her, hold her, pleasure her. Last night had been amazing, and he couldn't wait for a repeat. Sure, Xander had been with many partners before, but none of them had made him feel half as good as he did with Nef.

Xander met her outstretched hand with his own, and she nestled towards him until she was tucked against his chest again.

"We should explore the city today," Nef murmured sleepily. Her voice was deeper in the morning.

"Hmm," he kissed her forehead softly. "I would say yes, but we've received an alert about approaching sandstorms. Might be best to stay inside today."

"Oh nooooo," Nef said exaggeratedly. "I have to stay in bed with the sexiest man alive? Who happens to be naked? And hard as a rock?"

Xander blushed. He was, as she so delicately put it, hard as a rock, but he had been trying to lay down in such a way that he wouldn't, well, poke her.

"Somehow you don't strike me as too sad about the idea of being trapped in bed with me," he joked.

Nef rubbed at her eyes as she finally opened them, blinking a soft, coffee-rich gaze at him.

"I would never call being with you 'trapped', Xander."

Her eyes were wide, genuine, and Xander felt a tug in his chest. He leaned forward, kissing her deeply. How did this woman always know what to say? He hadn't even realised he had been worried she genuinely felt that way until she had denied it.

Nef wrapped her arms around Xander's neck and pulled him down on top of her. Hands on either side of her, Xander moaned as she tugged his hair lightly, ran her nails deliciously across his scalp.

Grinding against her, he slipped a hand down her chest to circle then tug lightly on one of Nef's nipples, eliciting a small whimper. Pleased, he did it again. Hearing Nef moan, watching her orgasm, only served to make him harder every time.

All of a sudden, Nef's hands were on his shoulders, pushing him onto his back. Surprised at the show of control, Xander let her manoeuvre him, watching her like a predator. He had an idea of what she wanted, but that didn't matter. She could ask for the stars in her palm and he would spend the rest of his life trying to make it happen.

Kneeling between his legs, she smiled like a fox in a chicken coop. Nef snaked her hand up his thigh, smiling wider as his cock twitched, pre-cum leaking from the tip. It was cute how smug Nef got when she thought she was in charge.

Cockily, Xander smirked at Nef and put his arms behind his head. He raised an eyebrow and nodded towards his groin, indicating for her to get on with it. He was rewarded with a mock scowl, then her hot mouth swallowing him down to the root.

"Shit," he gasped, burying his hands in the sheets. Eyes squeezed shut, he groaned loudly as she sucked audibly on him.

Opening his eyes, he watched as Nef worked her way around his bobbing member, wrapping both hands around him as she alternated between stroking his shaft and licking around the tip. The friction sent tingles through his body with every movement, and he clenched his teeth in an effort to not thrust his hips too hard.

Moving off him with a pop, Nef grinned wickedly. "Enjoying yourself, Sir?"

There was something about that term coming from her mouth that drove Xander crazy. He watched silently as Nef snaked her tongue out to lick the throbbing head of his cock, running it deliciously up and down his length before making a humming noise in her throat that made his balls tighten imperceptibly. Letting out a low groan of approval, Xander fisted her hair again, hard this time.

"Just like that honey," he murmured.

Bolstered, Nef wrapped her lips around him and took him deeper. God, her throat was so warm and tight and wet, a promise of where he would end up in a few short minutes if she kept this up. Nef shifted, gagging on his cock, sucking repeatedly in a smooth rhythm. Moaning, Xander lost himself briefly in the sensation of it all, giving in to the pleasure and thrusting his cock deeper down her throat.

Pulling off him and gasping for air, Nef continued to stroke him with both hands.

"Please Xander..." her lips were slightly parted, and her full breasts heaved with each breath she dragged in. "Please can you fuck me now?"

The pleading note in her voice was enough for Xander to turn his attention away from her nipples, which were currently hard, rosy peaks that he wanted to nibble on until she screamed.

"Hmm..." Xander sat up, tilted Nef's chin with a single finger before bringing his mouth close to her ear. "Beg better, and maybe I'll consider it."

Nef whimpered. More pre-cum was leaking from him now. He really hoped she begged, cause otherwise he was going to have to go back on his word and take her then and there.

"Please Xander," she inched closer. "Please fuck me. Please use me, make me scream."

Staying silent, Xander tilted his head. God, Nef had a mouth on her. He loved it.

Sensing that she needed to say more, Nef continued. "Please Sir. Please fuck me. I need your cock and I need you to make me yours."

Upon the last word, she flicked her tongue out again, swirling it around the tip of his cock and ending with a wet kiss pressed to his upper thigh.

Swearing, he pulled Nef down to him, giving her no time to balance before pushing her backwards onto the bed. Climbing after her, Xander bent her knees upwards towards her chest, hooking each ankle over his broad shoulders.

"Comfortable?" He whispered darkly. He needed to make sure she felt as good as he did.

"Very," Nef panted. "Now shut up and fuck me."

Amused, Xander dragged a finger between her legs, using the wetness he collected to stimulate her clit. As Nef opened her mouth to moan, he captured it with a searing kiss, simultaneously pushing two fingers into her.

"You're mine, Nef," he murmured against her mouth, hand starting a hard and fast thrusting rhythm. "And you're not in control here. So I'm not going to shut up, and I'm going to fuck you when I damn well please. And you're lucky I want to fuck you now, because otherwise I might leave you tied up here all afternoon without release."

Xander removed his hand and used it to gently grasp her throat. As he did, he shifted until he was lined up with her dripping pussy, and pressed forward to slide into her. As soon as they were fully joined, both let out a loud, long moan.

"Tell me what you are." Xander demanded as he started to thrust.

"Yours," gasped Nef. "I'm yours."

Growling his approval, Xander thrusted deep and lifted her hips higher for a better angle. Whimpering, Nef tried to shift against him and he reached that overly-sensitive spot inside her.

Soon, the sounds of skin on skin grew louder and more hurried. Xander ground against her, sucked on her neck, bit down lightly.

"Do you like it when I mark you like this?"

Nef's response was a garbled yes as she came for him, pussy quivering around his cock. He kept thrusting, prolonging her orgasm as much as possible.

And then Xander was spilling over, into her, whispering sweet nothings into her ear about how beautiful she is, how perfect, how her pussy was made for him and him alone. Finally spent, Xander collapsed on top of Nef.

"How is it," she said between heaving breathes, "you feel so *fucking* good every time?"

Xander laughed, turning so he could face Nef on the bed.

"I mean it," she said. "Plus, you're so attractive that every time we finish I feel like I'm ready to go another round."

Nef blushed a bit at her admission. She was adorable. And if she wanted more than one round, Xander was more than willing to oblige her.

"Don't worry honey," he whispered into her neck. "We're not done until I say we are."

CHAPTER 18

It had been two days of on and off sandstorms. Even though Nef knew she needed to finalise her exhibition blueprint and check in with her aunt about how the space was being cleared, she pushed her plans to the back of her mind, simply enjoying being spooned by Xander.

They hadn't touched their clothes in days. When room service came — and it came a lot — they simply threw on the complimentary bathrobes. Today was no different, and their robes sat pooled on the floor next to the tray of empty dishes.

Xander was running his hands soothingly across Nef's arms and stomach, and she made a low noise of contentment as she pulled the covers further up her body.

"I never want to leave," she sighed, rolling over and wrapping an arm across his muscled chest. T shirt tan lines were clearly visible, and Nef ran a finger across the V-shaped lines below his collarbones. She would love to see him in whatever shirt had made these marks.

Xander hummed in agreement. "Sandstorms are projected to finish up later today," he said quietly.

Nef stayed silent. No more sandstorms meant no more reason to stay here. Both of them needed to go home, move forward with their separate projects. She had already asked what suburb he lived in — her in Golden Hill, and Xander in Mission Hills, and while close, Xander had talked at length about his upcoming travel plans. Even if they were in the same state, it would only be for a few days, maybe a week, at a time. Nef didn't think she could stand to do long distance, not when it had no end date.

She rubbed absentmindedly at her chest, an ache starting up as she thought of the inevitable heartbreak. She might be willing to try a relationship — she was in too deep already — but was Xander on the same page? If he wanted to go their separate ways... what would she do? Was there even anything she could say without things moving too quickly?

A flick on her nose made her blink, Xander's concerned face coming into view. He was leaning over her on one elbow, brows furrowed.

"Talk to me, sweetheart. Something's bothering you."

"How could you tell?" Nef was curious. Was she really that obvious?

Xander smiled softly. "Your nose creases when you're thinking. It's adorable."

Nef blushed and bit her lip. Needing to move, she stood up and pulled on Xander's button down shirt, rumpled from being on the floor all night.

"Please talk to me, Nef." Xander got up as well, and Nef almost protested when he pulled on his briefs. "I want to take care of you. I can't do that unless I know what's wrong. Let me take care of you."

She should tell him. Finally ask for clarification about what they were. She had promised herself to talk about it before they went home, and now was as good a time as any.

When she opened her mouth, though, something else came out.

"What happened with your last relationship? What made you make your one night stand policy?"

Nef immediately wished she had never asked. Xander's face had gone pale. Sitting back down against the pillows, he cleared his throat and gripped the sheets with white knuckles. Cleared his throat again.

"I'm sorry if that was too nosy. You don't have to tell me anything you don't want to!" Nef blurted, heat rushing to her cheeks.

"No! No, I want to tell you. I just, um," Xander stumbled over his words. "I haven't talked about it. I mean to my therapist, but never to anyone else."

Nef latched onto the fact that he had a therapist. A mental image of a miniature Sophia dancing around Xander's head waving a green flag made her bite back a smile.

"You didn't even tell even Asim?" Nef was surprised. Weren't they best friends?

Xander shifted in his spot. If she didn't recognise that he needed space for this, she would have already been pressed against him, trying to soothe him with her touch.

"I don't talk to Asim about it," he said, "because he was there when it happened."

"It was 6 years ago now," Xander said. "I don't remember much of being 23, just that I had finally taken a break from travelling with my grandfather, and that staying in one location meant I could actually date a girl for more than a month at a time."

Jealousy sparked low in Nef's stomach. She hated the thought of Xander with someone else, but refused to examine that thought too closely yet.

"The girl in question was called Elissa. She was tall, dyed blonde, and very into fashion. We had been together for 10 months before it all went to pieces.

I thought I had prefaced my responsibilities from the start — Elissa knew I was doing my masters part time, knew I had plans to travel at the end of the year to start collecting again. She knew my grandfather gave me little choice, but I enjoyed my work so didn't mind. Most importantly, she knew how ambitious I was. Still am."

Xander glanced up at Nef then, seemingly trying to gauge her reaction. Nef squeezed his hand and scooted closer.

"I like your ambition," she murmured.

Smiling in thanks, Xander pressed a kiss to their entwined hands before continuing with his story.

They had spent months together in her childhood bedroom in her parent's place, where Xander would rant about his new ideas and goals. He had always wanted to fund his own dig, and he had been looking for buyers for a special bust of Aphrodite for months now. He had found it while diving off the coast of Chios; it was his first solo collection trip, and he felt immense pride at finding such an incredible piece. His grandfather, in a rare show of affection, had even ruffled his hair when he saw it.

Elissa had adored the bits and pieces of his collection that he had brought back with him. Some items had been as gifts, some just to show her before they were safely put on display in the family's gallery hall.

"And yes," he told Nef with an eye roll, "we actually did have a family gallery hall."

Elissa had always expressed admiration for the things he found, but in equal measure expressed her dislike of his need to travel so far for them. She didn't enjoy travel, and never accepted any of his offers to go on weekend trips interstate. She had never explained why, just given some vague excuse about being busy. But even though Xander now knew she hated when he left, hated that he had something in his life more important than her, he never considered it at the time.

The biggest regret he had, he thought, was that he hadn't ended it the first time he had had doubts. It had been nine months together at that point, and Xander had taken Elissa out for a nice dinner at a local restaurant in the city. Being young, and stupid, and a man, had decided that that would be the perfect time to tell her that he had found a buyer for his bust, who was willing to meet with him in just under a month. If the meeting was successful, he would have made enough of a profit to kickstart his very first dig, which he could *also* use as his base for a PhD, once his supervisor confirmed their interest. It would mean finally moving and living abroad, for however long he wanted. Out of the thumb of his grandfather for once.

He had been so excited. Too excited to notice how Elissa's smile wavered, how her voice was a bit too sweet when she congratulated him and asked where the meeting was. Too excited when he said it would be in Athens, and that he might end up starting his travel plans early so he wouldn't have to splurge on return tickets for in-between.

And when Elissa kept inquiring over the next month about exactly where, and when, and how the meeting would take place, Xander just thought she was equally excited for him. The perfect, supportive, interested girlfriend.

He was wrong.

Looking back on it, maybe he was at fault for some of it. He could have considered Elissa's feelings more, considered how him leaving early might feel like abandonment, especially when he hadn't even broken up with her or talked about if they were actually going to try be long distance. He hadn't really done or said anything in the end, and maybe that was half the problem. He had been too focused on his work, his job, that Elissa hadn't even been on the list of his priorities.

Regardless of the role he had played in his own self destruction, Xander, after months of therapy, knew that what happened next hadn't been his fault.

CHAPTER 19

Six years earlier, Athens

Xander had met his client at a vibrant, tucked away bar and restaurant in the main city. Live jazz had drifted through the open air room, and fragrant scents blew in and out from the kitchen at the back. The night had started so well, and his client was about to sign the papers for the transfer when Elissa had blown in like a hurricane, wobbling towards him on wafer thin heels.

Xander had stood up in alarm. Torn between helping her walk in a straight line and finishing his business meeting, he hovered frozen as she stumbled to their table.

"Alexander!" she had cried, practically falling into his arms.

Panicked, Xander had glanced around at the restaurant, heat rising to his cheeks as he saw people glance their way. Asim was a table away, his right hand man and best friend — steering clear for this meeting only, so Xander could properly do this sale alone. Asim moved to come help, but Xander had shaken his head subtly. This was his meeting. His circus, his monkeys.

"Elissa, what are you doing here?"

Her breath stunk of sour whiskey as she tried to kiss him sloppily. Moving his face out of the way, he held Elissa at arms length, nervously glancing at his client, who was watching with open curiosity.

"I came to help, silly!" Elissa giggled, and Xander's stomach tightened with nerves. He had a bad feeling about this.

"Elissa, please. Let me grab you a cab. I think we need to talk — let me finish my meeting?"

Xander tried to push Elissa towards the direction of the exit, but she gripped the lapel of his blazer, hiccuping.

"But I came to help you. You're making a mistake. You don't need to sell this stupid bust. You need to come home with me." Her words were starting to slur.

His client started to stand up. "Shall we finish this another time?"

"No! I mean, no, just give me a second, Rafa. My sincerest apologies."

Rafa sat back down, tapping his fingers impatiently on his wine glass.

"Elissa, please. You need to leave."

"No!" She whined petulantly.

"Elissa," Xander was exasperated now. "Please go. You can't be here right now. I don't even know how you got here. I thought you didn't drink!"

Anger twisted her features, an ugly expression taking over her face. Xander felt a rush of cold fear at what she was about to do. He had heard that Elissa could be vindictive, manipulative, but he had only heard of it from her distant acquaintances, never seen it. Now, he wished he hadn't ignored their warnings.

"You told me you were coming home," she pouted. "You said you'd sell the fake, then buy me that necklace you promised."

"What?" Shock rendered Xander speechless. What was she doing?

"Fake?" Rafa stood up again, chair scraping back loudly. Guests were starting to turn and watch them now. "What do you mean, fake?"

Elissa smiled sweetly, a mask to hide the rage Xander had glimpsed behind her eyes.

"Didn't he tell you? It's a fake. He had it copied, the real one is back home. I thought you knew."

"Rafa, please, she's lying!" Xander had never felt so ineloquent in his life.

Rafa shot him a disgusted look. "Deal is off, Mr Turner. Good luck finding a buyer."

Swiftly packing up, Rafa left in a huff. Restaurant patrons still stared at the trio. The realisation that Xander had failed hit like a truck, and he gripped the top of his chair for support. Self-hatred flooded him, along with fear of what his grandfather would do when he found out. He would weather whatever punishment was given, however. Anything to make sure his grandfather's wrath wasn't turned on his mother again.

"Oh, sugar," Elissa swayed closer, eyes hooded. "Surely you didn't think you would actually sell that lump of rock, did you?"

Xander shut his eyes tight. He didn't need this on top of everything. "You know that bust is real. Why did you do that?"

"That bust is a fake, sugar." Elissa made a sympathetic face, stroked his cheek.

"Please don't," Xander stepped back.

"Don't what?" She moved in closer still, hands now moving down his face to his chest, his stomach.

"Stop touching me, Elissa."

"I'm your girlfriend. I'm allowed to touch you. Just come home, we can catch the next flight out together."

"I'm leaving. I've already left. You shouldn't be here." Elissa kept moving closer, hands going to his belt now. Panic overtook him. This didn't feel real. What did he do with his hands?

Suddenly, Elissa gripped him between his legs, and Xander froze. Groping at him clumsily, Elissa was drawing horrified looks from those around them. Asim had stood up, furious, and was making his way towards them. No one else was moving to help.

"Come on, sugar. Come home with me. You didn't need that stupid deal. Come home," Elissa was ripping at his shirt, still squeezing his crotch.

Humiliated, Xander was grateful he at least wasn't hard. Did he push her away? He didn't want to hurt her. But this… the realisation slapped him in the face as his body went numb. He didn't want this.

He wanted to run, to scald himself with hot water and wash away her touch. He felt like he was ready to throw up, but his throat wasn't working.

"Stop," he whispered. He couldn't seem to speak past a lump in his throat.

"What was that, sugar?" Elissa was slurring, was pulling buttons off his top now, exposing his chest. She flicked at his exposed nipple, and shame enveloped him.

Before she could keep going, before Xander could crawl into a pit and die, Asim was there, dragging Elissa off him with a death stare so powerful it made Xander cringe.

Finally able to move, Xander slowly backed away towards the door, trying not to meet anyones eyes. As Asim started yelling at Elissa, demanding the restaurant manager call the police, Xander turned and ran out into the night.

Xander never attempted a face to face sale again. Instead, refusing to let Elissa win, he started his auctions.

"Nef? You haven't said anything yet and I'm getting worried. Shit, did this trigger something for you? I'm so sorry, I should have asked first."

Nef's heart was aching for him. This sweet, confident, successful man had gone through what she considered to be one of her worst nightmares. Reaching out to cup his face, she pressed their foreheads together.

"Xander," she whispered. "Why on earth are you apologising? I don't even know what to say. I can't believe you've been carrying that burden for so long."

A breath shuddered out of him. "I didn't realise how much I wanted to tell you."

Pressing a soft kiss to the corner of his mouth, Nef ran a hand through his hair, playing with the soft auburn strands.

"Thank you for telling me."

Relaxing, Xander leant back against the pillows again, pulling Nef into his side.

"Long story aside, I get the feeling my last relationship wasn't what was actually bothering you." He gave her a sly look, and Nef bit her lip. Caught. How did he know her so well already?

"Fine," she sighed. Her turn to sit up now, she crossed her legs and pulled the doona over her like a cape.

Time to be honest. What did she have to lose? Xander, the little voice whispered to her from the back of her mind. You could lose Xander.

Nef shoved that voice deep down inside her. She may not have been in many relationships, but she knew enough to know that that fear never went away. If she lived her whole life trying to keep someone, she'd never end up enjoying the time she had with them. She'd just waste away with her own worries, until the person she loved ended up dead, or gone.

Like her mother. Maybe if Nef had appreciated her more while she was still alive, she wouldn't have held on for so long afterwards. Maybe if she hadn't been so focused on keeping her mom on life support, she would have been able to use those first few months to find the courage to say goodbye properly.

A quote floated to her conscience: 'tis better to have loved and lost, than never to have loved at all'. Alfred Lord Tennyson. Aunty Tiye had requested that be the quote put on her mom's gravestone. A stupid cliche, she had thought at the time. It still was, but now she understood.

Taking a deep breath, Nef finally confessed.

CHAPTER 20

"I'm worried that because we're likely going home tomorrow, that even though this wasn't technically a one night stand, that you don't want to see me again."

Xander blinked at Nef's bluntness. Damn. He liked that she was so straightforward. No games — unless it was in the bedroom.

Nef kept speaking. "I'm mostly worried because I know that *I* really want to keep seeing you. I know we said we'd take it slow, but I want a label. I don't casually see people. I won't push you for all or nothing, but I can't make an exception for you just because you're not comfortable committing."

"Ouch," Xander pressed a hand to his chest in mock betrayal.

Nef's lips were red from where she was nibbling at them nervously. Combined with the way she clutched the sheets around her, how his shirt was riding up her naked thighs, and how she simultaneously stared him down with impressive regal-ness, Xander was having trouble deciding if he wanted to laugh, respond, or kiss her first.

Before he could do anything, Nef playfully whacked him with a pillow. How did she even move that fast?

"You have to say something, damnit! I'm baring my soul here." Nef was grinning, but Xander could see the tension in her eyes.

His dick won the battle first. Surging forward and grabbing the pillow before its next attack, Xander kissed Nef deeply, licking into her mouth and biting her full bottom lip. When her arms came up to envelope him, he pulled back slightly, breathing heavily.

"Nef." Xander panted, kissed her again. He didn't think there were words to fully express how much he wanted to see her again. "Nef, if I don't see you again, touch you again, after tonight, I think I'll die of starvation."

He swallowed her thrilled gasp with another kiss, desperation filling his veins. He didn't care how they would make it work. He didn't care if he could only grab a few stolen moments in between his trips. He wanted to try. He wanted to keep this woman who made him feel lighter.

Nef had the sense to care, though. Pulling out of his reach, shirt halfway up her stomach and hair sexily mussed, she put a hand on his chest to stop him from following her to the edge of the bed.

"Wait," she gasped out. Pushing her curls out of her eyes, she wriggled back into a cross legged position. "I want to make sure this works — for both of us. I have questions."

Xander scowled. "Questions can wait, Nef. Your pussy can't. Let me taste you. Now."

Nef made a low noise in her throat, pressing her lips together. "How about this: questions first, then I'm yours all night."

Xander raised an eyebrow. God, he was aching for her. Only his queen would make such demands when he could be on his knees for her by now. His queen. Nef would be his. A warm, bubbly feeling fizzed in his stomach. He wanted that. To call her his. Thoughts of Nef filled his mind: showing her his new museum, maybe offering her a job as curator at one of his next digs so she could travel with him, him introducing her as his girlfriend —

The word clanged through him, dragging ice shards up his insides. Xander could have screamed. He hated feeling like this. The idea of that label, even now... He knew Nef was different. She definitely wasn't Elissa. But every time he thought long term, he felt like he was standing on a cliff, ready to be kicked over. Could he really be sure that Nef wouldn't be a repeat in 10 months?

His mind ticked forward at a hundred miles a minute. Maybe, if he waited until after he finalised the museum sale, he could see that it would be different. Not just think it would be, but actually feel ready. It would be his first face to face sale since the first attempt, and if that went well, surely it would be a sign?

Swallowing hard, Xander shifted back so he was sitting properly on the edge of the bed.

"Questions first," he agreed. "But you should know I… I can't call you my girlfriend yet."

Just saying the word aloud made him feel like he had sucked on a lemon.

"I don't mean that I don't want to eventually," he rushed on as Nef's face fell. God, she was an open book. He hated being the one to put that expression on her face. "I just… I need more time."

Nef smiled, and Xander wanted to melt into the blankets in pure relief.

"Of course," she breathed. "I told you, I don't want all or nothing, I just want you. And, well, if I'm being honest, I want a promise that you won't see anyone else while you're seeing me."

Smug satisfaction filled his chest knowing she seemed to be just as jealous as he was.

"I promise, Nef. Just you." Nef's eyes flashed joyfully, and Xander felt another thrill go through him at knowing he had caused that happiness.

"Although, maybe I might want someone else to join us in the bedroom…"

It was clearly a joke, but Xander felt that now-familiar flood of jealousy in the pit of his stomach.

Scowling, he gripped a fistful of Nef's hair at the base of her spine, tugging lightly. Nef moaned, and Xander leant forward to whisper in her ear.

"I don't share, sweetheart. If you're really craving to be filled in more than one way, I'll buy you a vibrator. Understood?"

A shiver ran down Nef's spine, and she whimpered.

"So not including this vibrator… we're exclusive?" Nef was up on her knees now, and it was taking all his concentration to focus on her words and not the way she looked in his shirt.

"Yes, Nef," Xander dragged his knuckles across her thigh. "We're exclusive. I might not be able to see you in person for the first few weeks though, at least until I finalise my latest project."

He felt bad starting their relationship this way, but work had to come first. Always.

Nef shuffled closer, letting him drag his hand further up her legs, fingertips brushing under the hem of her shirt. Higher.

"There's always phone sex," she smirked.

Xander burst into laughter. This was already going better than expected.

The airport was surprisingly crowded for a 10pm flight to San Diego, but fortunately for Nef, she was with Xander. Who she often forgot was a millionaire.

"You don't just have a private jet?" She playfully nudged him where he sat next to her on the couch, thighs touching. They were in the private lounge, and had already been served bubbling glasses of champagne and small side dishes.

"No way," Xander looked indignant. "The emissions of those things? I can fly in style AND do my bit to save the planet at the same time."

Nef smiled and rested her head on his shoulder. It was so humid despite the blasting air con, and her hair tickled the back of her neck where it sat in a thick low bun. She almost regretted her denim shorts and short sleeved, cropped orange button shirt, but she knew San Diego would be nearly as hot when they got home.

After their earlier conversation, the rest of the day had disappeared in a blur of architecture and eating. The sandstorms had finished as projected, their flight was changed without issues, and they had managed to visit a few of the more famous tourist traps before heading to the airport. Nef had loved seeing Xander outside of work, but she was also excited to see him start this new project of his. There was something really sexy about a man who could dominate a room, and Xander at the auction had had a presence that made her whole body tingle. She wanted to see more of it, even if she couldn't see him in person for a few weeks.

Xander hadn't told her much about his project when she had asked, just that he wanted to start up a new event space as another form of income to fund his future digs. He was negotiating a deal for a piece of land (he hadn't said where; it was likely on the outskirts of San Diego, Nef imagined) and once complete, he would decide whether to renovate and refurnish the existing building or whether he would demolish and rebuild entirely.

Stretching out an arm around her, Xander tugged gently on a loose curl. "I've organised for a car to pick you up when we land."

"Oh! Thank you." Nef said in surprise. She had naively thought they might get a cab together, might go back to his before heading home properly. "Are you coming as well?"

"I need to head straight to my office to pick up some documents and finalise some accounts now that the auction is over. Sorry sweetheart."

Xander seemed distracted, but his apology felt genuine.

"You sure you don't want to drive with me to the office? I live on the way to the city centre, after all."

Xander blinked at her, as though pulling himself back to the present.

"My office is in New York," he winced. Nef's heart sank. She would have loved just a couple more minutes with him. Despite them now being exclusive, all sorts of doubts filled her head at thoughts of what might happen when they weren't in the same building. It was stupid and Nef knew it, but tell that to her subconscious.

As though sensing her mood, Xander slid his hand around the back of her neck and drew her in for a long, slow kiss that heated her straight to her core.

Breaking apart breathlessly, he peppered a few more kisses on her cheek, the tip of her nose, her forehead. Nef laughed at his antics, pleased that he wasn't the kind of guy to shy away from PDA.

Looking at her with those bedroom eyes of his, Nef flushed as he slowly dragged his gaze down then back up her body.

"Follow me," his deep voice rumbled through her chest.

A stupid request, really. Nef would follow him to the ends of the earth. And from the way he cockily grinned at her, she was worried he might already know it.

CHAPTER 21

Nef was confused when Xander led her to the private bathrooms, a secluded, dimly lit marble and tile modern monstrosity located down a hall at the back. When he dragged her furtively into the women's rooms, pushing her quickly into a single cubicle, realisation lit up her body like fireworks.

"Xander," she whispered frantically, "here? What if people come in?"

"Is that your only concern? Getting caught? Cause if not, we can stop right now. It's your call."

Nef hesitated, thinking for a second. "I think getting caught is my only concern. But… the idea of this is pretty hot," she admitted.

"Easy solution, sweetheart," Xander whispered back. "You just have to stay quiet."

Xander barely let her finish agreeing before he was pressing her against the back of the cubicle door, kissing her roughly. All Nef's thoughts melted away as she got lost in the taste of him, the feel of his hard biceps caging her in place.

Xander groaned against her mouth. "You taste so fucking good, Nef. So sweet."

Nef moaned as he started unbuckling her belt, her own hands fumbling as she started to return the favour. She needed him inside her desperately.

Finally getting his slacks open, she reached for his underwear — which wasn't there. Not that she was complaining, of course. Looking at him questioningly, Xander shrugged with a chagrined smile.

"I was waiting to do laundry until I got back. Had to get creative."

Amused, Nef stroked him slowly, recapturing his mouth with her own. Tongues brushing lazily against each other, Nef pressed closer, the friction of his chest against her shirt and bra stimulating her sensitive nipples.

Suddenly, Xander's hands were on her hips, twisting her around and forcing her to brace her hands on the door. Rough calluses brushed the tops of her hips, her thighs, as he dragged her shorts and underwear down in one smooth movement.

The cold air against her nether region made Nef gasp, and Xander quickly put a hand over her mouth to silence her.

"Shhh sweetheart," he murmured as he slid a finger up and down her entrance. Removing his hand from her mouth, he started playing with her breasts, teasing her nipples into hard peaks.

Nef knew she was soaking wet, and Xander was taking full advantage of it as he prepared her for his cock. She was lightly thrusting her hips now in time with his fingers, and flashes of their time in that shed just over a week ago threatened to make her finish before she wanted to.

"Xander," Nef held back a whimper. "Please, I don't want to finish yet."

"I didn't realise you got a choice," Xander's voice was low with lust and the need for quiet as he added another finger.

Shaking with restraint and the need to be filled by him, Nef leant forward, simultaneously grinding her ass back into Xander's crotch. She wasn't going to break first.

"*God*, your ass is amazing. If we weren't in a public restroom I'd make you crawl to me."

Xander slowly pressed a third finger into her, making her feel deliciously full. Her focused narrowed to his talented ministrations, and it took her a second to remember what he had said.

"*Make* me crawl to you? Not likely, Alexander."

Xander gave a low laugh that sent a thrill through her stomach.

"You're right, sweetheart. I won't make you. You'll beg to."

Desire rippled through her. He was absolutely right. And if he kept up the way he was now circling her clit, she would be begging pretty soon.

Xander loved making Nef come undone. He wanted to record her when she came, watch her face on repeat as her eyes fluttered, sinful full lips parting, pussy clamping down on his fingers.

As Nef braced herself against the cubicle door with shaky legs, Xander brought his fingers, coated in her, up to her mouth.

"Open," he ordered.

Obediently, Nef opened her mouth, swirling her tongue over the pads of his fingers in a way that somehow made Xander even harder.

A small moan escaped him at the sight of her slightly bent, legs spread at the knees, her pussy glistening. Hurrying, reached into his pocket and grabbed a condom from his wallet, rolling it on deftly.

Lining himself up with her core, Xander pushed in hard, swearing as he finally sunk into her centre. He would never get over how tight she was, how perfectly she meld to the shape of him.

Made for each other, Xander thought as he started thrusting, reaching a hand around them to keep teasing Nef's sensitive nub.

They didn't speak. They didn't need to. Their bodies moved together in sync, and Xander lost himself in the feel of her soft skin, her warm body. Silently, he thanked whatever god for keeping the bathroom empty, especially as the sounds of skin against skin got louder.

Burying his head in the crook of Nef's neck to silence his groans of pleasure, he tangled his hands in her low bun. Tugging lightly, he skimmed a knuckle over her clit once more, feeling immense satisfaction as Nef let out a cry of ecstasy and came again.

Moving faster now, he pounded into Nef, gripping her hips hard enough to leave fingerprints.

"Oh god, Xander, don't stop," Nef begged. "I need you to come for me."

He was ruined. He had never had someone match his pace in bed before — or in this case, in the bathroom. Everything he wanted to give Nef, she wanted to take, and he wanted to give her the world.

Shuddering, he thrust once more then held still, gripping Nef tightly as her legs quivered. She was panting, small breathy sounds that threatened to make him hard again.

"If you're a good girl for me on the flight back, maybe I'll let you come again."

Nef made a low sound in her throat and dropped her head onto her arms, still supporting herself against the door. Always adorable. How was he supposed to go three weeks without her? Punctuating his promise with a kiss to the top of Nef's spine, he slowly withdrew from her, and they both pulled their clothes back into place.

Perfect timing, because just then the intercom chimed from overhead, calling their flight.

Letting herself in with the spare key, Nef texted her aunt to let her know she was home and that she would see her in the morning. It was late, and Nef didn't want to wake Aunty Tiye up for no reason, especially when she was barely sleeping at the moment with the stress of selling the museum and her new job.

The car ride had been quiet. Nef had spent the drive reminiscing about the last two weeks. It hadn't been that long, but Nef had never fallen so hard and fast for someone. She couldn't wait to meet up with Sophia later this week, tell her all about Xander's tender kiss goodbye and promise to call her when he reached his office.

Cheesy though it was, and although she knew Sophia would tease her relentlessly, knowing that Xander wanted to make this work made her giddy with happiness. Holding on to that feeling, Nef struggled out of her clothes and dragged herself to the bathroom down the hall to shower and change, grabbing her favourite ratty tie dye shirt for pjs.

Nef emerged from the steam twenty minutes later and padded back to her room slowly, hair wrapped gracefully in a towel. She was grateful to no longer smell like plane and travel sweat. Glaring at her suitcase propped in the corner of her room, she silently willed it to unpack itself. Naturally, it didn't, so Nef compromised and flopped into bed, leaving it for the morning. She was too tired to even dry her hair properly, and would probably need to wash it again tomorrow. Oh well, she thought. Sleep is for the weak, and she was definitely weak right now.

If she closed her eyes though, would the last two weeks turn out to have just been a dream? Nef knew she was being fanciful, knew she could just check her phone and see evidence of Xander's brief text to her, telling her he had boarded and hoped she had gotten home ok. Before she could worry herself further though, exhaustion caught up to her and she drifted off to sleep.

CHAPTER 22

The museum was busy, and Nef's sensory overload was starting to grate on her. She had spent the past week alternating between meeting with builders, interior designers, and fellow museum staff to coordinate her exhibition, which would take place in the main left wing — after a lot of changes.

Nef had wanted to create an elegant, interactive space to mimic the design in the Acropolis Museum in Athens. Pedestals would be set up at carefully calculated angles, so each piece would be strategically seen from each angle as the guests walked through. The exhibition would flow into a narrower and narrower space, culminating in Xander's auction master piece, set up in a dazzling glass chamber like Nefertiti's Bust. And through the whole exhibit, dim lighting and tiny fairy lights to mimic stars would wrap around olive and laurel trees, creating a living ancient garden inside the building. Aunty Tiye had said the concept reminded her of a cross-over between the gardens from the Disney movies 'Hercules' and 'Aladdin'. Nef wasn't mad about that comparison.

Her blueprint binder was getting thicker and thicker though, and with every change or reevaluation, Nef's headache grew. Even texting Xander between meetings was stressful. Not because of him, but because she felt bad that she was so busy she could only talk for a few minutes at a time. Even in the evenings, she was swept away in a whirlwind of her friends, Sophia, or her aunt, all eager to hear about her adventures, her romance, and her upcoming show. Her only comfort was that she knew Xander was just as busy, sorting out his new project and simultaneously planning future digs and managing old ones. She wondered if he would do another auction soon. If this exhibition of hers took off, she'd need a reliable business partner to supply her with artifacts...

Nef really needed to just block out a time to call Xander properly. She missed him, but was too nervous to tell him yet. She probably could, she thought to herself. From the second he had touched down in New York, he had sent her constant updates — a nice change from men who would either ghost her or text her one word responses. Instead, Xander had been sending her paragraphs, photos, and (as of two days ago) an enormous bouquet of deep red roses, which she kept displayed in a vase on the pedestal in her exhibition hall that would eventually hold Thuya's death mask.

Smiling softly at the vase at the end of the hall, the sounds of enthusiastic tourists and clamouring tradesmen faded to a light buzz as Nef's phone dinged with a text.

I MISS YOU, it read.

Grinning, Nef felt a blush creep over her cheeks as a photo popped up, showing Xander seated low in his desk chair, black buttoned shirt tight in all the right places, piercing blue eyes seemingly gazing at her from through the screen. God, he was gorgeous. Nef couldn't look at him without feeling a mix of desire and longing, and the reminder that Xander would be away for a few more weeks made her chest ache. She knew that a single hug from him would soothe all her nerves amongst the commotion of the museum, even though it had only been a few short weeks.

Biting her lip, Nef's fingers sped across the keys in response.

I MISS YOU TOO. I WAS JUST THINKING ABOUT YOU.

Another photo. This time not of Xander, but of his desk: opaque glass, clear of everything but his laptop and a single red rose in a tall vase in the corner.

I'M ALWAYS THINKING ABOUT YOU. I WANT TO GIVE YOU THE NEXT BOUQUET IN PERSON, he sent.

Gesturing to her fellow workers — technically, her employees for now — she excused herself. Leaving the left wing, she power-walked to the back hall of the museum (the Asia-Pacific display) and ducked into a crowded but now-unused storage room.

Finally breathing freely in the silence and company of ancient artifacts, Nef leaned against the back of the door and grabbed her phone again. Xander had sent more messages.

I CAN'T WAIT TO BE IN THE SAME ROOM AS YOU. THE SAME BED. I MISS SMELLING YOUR PERFUME ON MY PILLOW IN THE MORNING.

She wanted that so badly. Each night when she finally collapsed into bed in Aunty Tiye's two-bedroom apartment, she texted Xander until her vision blurred, then teased herself to an orgasm while thinking of him before falling asleep. The memory of their nights together wouldn't be enough forever though, and was barely enough to satisfy her now. Nef needed Xander in person, to touch him, kiss him, hold him. She hadn't realised how touch starved she had been until those last few weeks, how much she had loved being held, cherished.

CAN WE CALL SOON? PROPERLY? I MISS YOUR VOICE, Nef texted back.

His response was instant.

I GET OFF WORK AT 10PM. I'LL CALL YOU. DON'T WEAR UNDERWEAR.

Nef was grateful she was hidden away in the storeroom, because she was sure her face couldn't be more red, or her underpants more drenched. She typed out a short response, cheeks hurting from smiling so hard.

Reenergised, she slipped her phone back into her pocket and bounced back to the left wing, ready to get back to work.

Drumming his fingers on his thigh, Xander stood behind his faux-leather chair staring out at the silhouette of the Empire State Building. It was almost six, and Xander kept a strict policy about never working past his allocated hours. He may be the director of his company, but Asim was CEO. He'd leave the long hours to him.

Wednesdays meant drinks with his colleagues, usually at one of the nearby rooftop bars they had been frequenting for years. Part of him wanted to go, didn't want to change his routine. The other part of him wanted to rush home and call Nef already. A few days had passed since their first proper phone call, and since then, it had unintentionally become a nightly routine to call each other before they went to sleep.

During the day, they were constantly messaging each other, the texts also a source of constant arousal. It hadn't been great for his business meetings. However, he had managed to get through this week. Just because he had used Zoom a lot more than usual didn't mean anything.

"You coming, Xander?" Josh, a tall lanky colleague who was in charge of the financial aspects of his company, was standing in the doorway of his office.

Making up his mind, Xander forced himself to be patient. And to not think of Nef. Or how he wished she was joining him for drinks, her underwear tucked in his pocket. He cleared his throat.

"Wouldn't miss it," he flashed Josh a grin. Together, they headed to the elevators, joined by Declan and a few others from different departments.

Technically, this office and the company were his grandfather's, left to him after his death. Xander had loved the work but hated the man, and had immediately stepped down as CEO, leaving it to Asim. Despite only being a department head, Asim always told Xander his plans first, and didn't like doing anything without his approval. Xander hadn't liked it initially, but his ambition had soon gotten the better of him. Despite the blurring of lines between their jobs, Asim and Xander had worked together to spur their organisation into a large multimillion dollar company, where they bought, sold, and funded various archeological events, explorations, museums, and charities.

Now, they had various employees in charge of multiple departments, with roles including assisting with writing tourism policies in ancient sites such as Pompeii, to organising the auctions.

While Xander was officially the director of excavations, he floated in between everything and was considered the networker of the company. Events like the auction, even tonight with weekly drinks, were less social events and more just informal ways to meet new sponsors or business partners.

Sighing impatiently, Xander checked his phone again as the group piled into the lift. Smiling, he opened the picture Nef had sent him: a slightly blurry photo of an empty museum wing, tradesmen carrying wooden planks and drills in the background, her friend and colleague Zara looking like she was in a heated conversation with one of them. The text beneath the photo made him laugh.

*SHE MAY BE 5 FOOT 2 BUT SHE WILL FIGHT YOU!
DON'T COME BETWEEN ZARA AND HER BLUEPRINTS.*

Nef had told him about her coworkers, many of whom had also been there since she started working. Zara, if he remembered correctly, was her favourite: a tiny, petite, thirty five year old woman with a sharp blonde bob and an even sharper tongue. She had studied interior design, and was a master with blueprints; she was the one making Nef's ideas come to life.

The elevator dinged, and the group stepped into the lobby. Before they reached the doors, one of the receptionists called out Xander's name.

"Xander!" He didn't recognise her. She must be new, and she wobbled towards him on sky high black stilettos, the shoes making uneven clicking sounds on the marble floor. Finally reaching him, she held out a thick cream envelope.

"This arrived in the mail for you today," she breathed.

Xander nodded absently, accepting the letter. The textured paper had his full first name written across it in neat calligraphy, swooping lines of black ink punctuated with a fancy underline. He frowned. He didn't think he knew anyone with such nice handwriting.

"Thanks," he told the receptionist. Turning around, he motioned to the group at the door, now joined by Tina and Alexandra (who went by Alex, thankfully), employees from the human resources and marketing department respectfully.

"I'll catch up!" Xander called. He quickly walked back to the elevator, where he rode to the first floor and hid in one of the now-empty meeting rooms. For some reason, he didn't want to open the letter in front of everyone, and he didn't want to wait until he was home.

Holding up the envelope again, Xander realised it was scented — he just couldn't place what. Opening it with a single crisp movement, he pulled out a thick folded piece of paper in a matching cream colour. Unfolding it, the same black calligraphy formed a paragraph in the centre of the page.

The sound of your voice is rich, full like the taste of date wine and I, drunken girl in a tangle of flowers live only a captive to hear it.

A bright red lipstick mark decorated the bottom right as a signature. Bringing the letter closer, he sniffed at the paper, then grinned. It was Nef's signature citrus and vanilla scent.

Chest warm, he carefully refolded the paper and stored the envelope in his blazer pocket before heading back to the lobby. He didn't have the words yet to say thank you. But as the scent of her perfume lingered, it gave him an idea.

CHAPTER 23

Sophia sat next to Nef on her beat up red couch, sun streaming in from the single large window on the wall to their left. Silent, they stared at the several large packages that sat on the wooden coffee table, obscuring the tv on the wall opposite them.

"How many boxes did he send again?" Sophia's voice was faint with shock.

Nef had to swallow once, twice, before she could speak.

"Seven."

Soph's sandy coloured, fluffy hair floated in a cloud around her as she stood from the couch and flipped open the lid of one of the boxes.

"He is one rich bitch, Nef. Marry him, or I will."

"Soph!" Nef spluttered.

"I'm joking, obviously! I have Eliot. But Nef, a man who buys every single bottle of your signature perfume in stock IN THE COUNTRY, then somehow convinces the manufacturers to stop producing it, *solely for the purpose* because he likes you and doesn't want anyone else smelling like you? I don't know if I'm scared scared, or scared amazed. The flag is currently very beige."

Nef choked on a strained laugh. This felt like too much. Stuff like this didn't happen to her. To anyone. Surely extravagant gifts like this were reserved for books like Fifty Shades. Feeling herself start to panic, she cradled her head between her knees.

"Is it possible to feel imposter syndrome about a relationship?" Nef wheezed out to Sophia.

Digging through her tote bag, Sophia found her asthma puffer and offered it to Nef. Shrugging it away, Nef pulled herself up and headed to the kitchen down the hall, pouring then downing a glass of water in one go. She was tempted to pour a second glass over her head. Anything to cool the growing anxiety in her bones.

Soph rounded the small island and removed her glasses before pulling Nef into a proper hug. Taller than her friend, Nef buried her face in Soph's hair, relaxing slowly as Soph rubbed her back comfortingly.

"You've had such shitty luck with men before, honey. Maybe you've finally found someone who'll treat you like your namesake — like the queen you are."

Nef thought back to the note that had accompanied the first box.

"To my queen," it had started. "No-one else gets to smell as delicious as you. Can't wait to have you back in my bed soon. X."

The thing was, she loved how attentive and generous Xander was being. Yes, extravagantly so, but who wouldn't love being treated this way? Nef just worried that this wouldn't last. That he'd tire of their exclusivity, wouldn't be able to take the next step, or any step. She was already in too deep with her feelings. What if she got too used to this?

Sophia had gone back to the living room and was now spraying herself with a bottle of perfume from the top box. Giving Nef a sly look, she squirted another puff down the collar of her shirt.

"I figured I could use some. You know, considering you have *every single one* in America now."

Rubbing her temples, Nef sighed and gave in to Soph's teasing. Grabbing the bottle from her best friend, she sprayed her wrists, dabbed some behind her ears. She guessed there wasn't really a need to be liberal with it now, plus the added bonus of saving about two hundred bucks a year.

"You should drop some hints to Eliot," Nef said with a smile. "Tell him to up his game."

Soph laughed, red staining her pale cheeks. Biting her lip, she wrung her hands together.

"Actually," she murmured. "He's planning to buy me something a bit more valuable."

Nef froze. Was this what she thought Soph was talking about?

"Soph," she warned. "Don't tease me. Spill."

A wide grin split Sophia's face as she finally met Nef's gaze.

"He asked me to go ring shopping with him. I said duh!"

Squealing, Nef launched herself at Sophia, jumping up and down as she grasped her by the shoulders.

"That's so exciting! Finally! Oh my GOD Soph I'm so happy for you!!!" Nef could have cried. Soph may have been waiting for this forever, but Nef had been waiting equally as long to see her friend get her happily ever after.

"Ok ok coffee's on me! We have spicy details to share. Will Eliot kill me if I offer to do some preliminary shopping with you?"

Sophia laughed. "Absolutely. But you do need to help me choose my outfit for when he actually asks."

Heart bursting with happiness, Nef grabbed Sophia's arm and led her out of the apartment. It was good to be home.

Xander loved his New York bedroom. This whole apartment, really. Not as much as he loved his townhouse in San Diego, but a very close second.

Towelling his hair dry as he left his ensuite, he emerged through his walk in wardrobe to the actual bedroom. The bedroom door stood opposite the door to the wardrobe, and he had to turn a corner to see the bed. His king sized bed sat against the wall that hid the wardrobe/ensuite area, and was made up with a plush wine coloured doona and matching pillow. Two gunmetal bedside tables (to match the accent wall) sat on either side, one laden with a lamp, a pile of books, and his reading glasses, and the other with lush green plants that trailed over the side. The bed faced his favourite part of his room though: floor to ceiling windows, framed by thick grey curtains, curved outwards like the edge of a fishbowl.

Currently, the view was a sea of sparkling lights, slightly obscured on the right by the neighbouring apartment building. Fortunately, he was high up enough, and facing away from the other building, that he wasn't self conscious about standing there in the light of his lamp in just a pair of navy briefs.

Xander checked his watch, which he had tossed on his bed before his shower, next to his laptop. Quarter past ten. Almost time to call Nef. He grinned, anticipation buzzing through him, his cock standing to attention just thinking of her. Drawing the curtains half-closed, he dove under the covers and opened the computer.

He hoped Nef liked his gift. He really, really hoped he hadn't scared her off. She had texted him an all-caps thank you with a ton of exclamation marks and a red heart, but he didn't exactly have any siblings - or his mom - to ask what that meant. It seemed positive? Asim, as usual, had been useless, and there was no way he was going to ask Declan or Erik.

Music chimed loudly, and Xander rushed to answer the call.

"Nef! Wow, you look gorgeous." Xander knew he was smiling too widely to look sane, but he didn't care. He wanted to reach through the screen and kiss her.

"Thanks, Xander," Nef laughed shyly.

She did look gorgeous. A black tank top, showing off her ample cleavage, hair out in loose curls, makeup in what he now knew was her signature — wing swept eyeliner and deep red lips he wanted pressed against his chest. Lower. Her eyes roved down the screen, taking in his bare torso, chiseled and still dotted with a few water drops. Definitely not intentional. He definitely hadn't made sure to go to the gym later than usual today, and shower immediately after. Purely coincidence. She bit her lip, and Xander's cock hardened again immediately. It was Xander's turn to feel shy, though.

"So you liked my gift?" His voice was low, quiet.

Nef breathed out something between a laugh and sigh. "I loved it. Xander, I really did. Thank you. You know just one bottle would have been more than enough though, right?"

Almost floating with relief, Xander leant back against the pillows and subtly flexed an arm behind his head.

"I know it would have been enough. But you deserve the world. I told you, remember? Let me take care of you."

Nef grinned, visibly chuffed. She was sitting on a small two seater couch, and as she shifted to put her legs up he caught sight of the boxes of perfume he had sent her piled on the low coffee table in front of her. Good. Seeing her happy, comfortable, with things he had provided for her, made him surprisingly proud and content.

They kept talking, trading stories about their day. Nef was beyond excited for her friend's imminent engagement, and Xander updated her about his latest plans for another dig sometime next year — Tunisia this time. Somehow, Josh had found the budget to send over someone to scout the area, and his night out the other day had helped them bump into a willing sponsor.

An hour ticked by, and Nef had retreated to her bedroom. Changing into pyjamas off-camera (to Xander's disappointment), he took the time to snoop as much as he could at her room.

Her double bed had an ivory frame and was propped against a clean white wall, a small window with pull-down blinds above it. The edge of his screen showed a simple white armoire with a dressing gown hung over the knob, and the room was accented in shades of black, cream, and orange. It was very Nef — elegant, tasteful, coordinated. He imagined she had a desk on the wall he couldn't see, covered with plans for her exhibition.

Nef came back into frame, and Xander's heart nearly stopped. She wore a faded tie dye top cropped to just above her navel. *Only* that faded tie dye top.

Fuck me, he thought.

CHAPTER 24

"Last time you were disappointed when I wore underwear." Nef's smile was sizzling, lips still that deep red Xander loved so much.

It was true. But he understood — she hadn't been ready to try phone sex. And he, more than most, would rather die than pressure her into anything. Clearing his throat, he settled deeper into his pillows. She was evidently ready tonight.

"I'm not disappointed now," he rumbled. Far from it. He hadn't thought he could even get this hard without Nef being physically next to him. He was wrong.

Nef did a slow twirl, and Xander's mouth went dry. The things he wanted to do to her right now... Nef knew. Of course she knew. He fucking loved that she knew, that as she faced him again she pushed herself back onto her sheets, keeping the camera propped up at the foot of the bed so he had a full view of her as she spread her legs slowly and ran a hand slowly down, then up, her naked thigh. She had put on wireless headphones, he noticed, and he was grateful because her next words were quiet.

"Tell me if you want me to stop," she whispered, hand moving dangerously close to her centre.

"If you stop," Xander clenched his teeth as Nef split herself open with a finger, showing him how drenched she already was. "If you stop, I won't let you finish."

"Oh?" Nef raised an eyebrow, sunk a finger deep into her core with a soft groan. Xander's cock twitched. "What if I stop anyway?"

His perfect, spoiled brat. Xander loved it when she got like this.

"I won't let you, Nef."

"Make me, *Sir*."

That did it. Xander placed his laptop at the end of the bed and quickly stripped out of his briefs. He was aching, pre-cum already forming at the end of his throbbing member.

Nef was staring at him, biting her lip again. Xander grabbed a tube of lube from the drawer of his bedside table, not taking his eyes off Nef.

"Tell me what to do," Nef breathed. "Do you want me to use my fingers?"

"Do you have other options?"

Nef nodded, and reached into the draw of her bedside table.

"This one's my favourite," she grinned.

Holding it up for him to see, she held a red silicone rabbit vibrator. He had seen them before, but never being used. This one was an average size, but thick and curved at the tip. Almost mimicking his own.

"It vibrates?" Xander was nearly vibrating with excitement himself. He desperately wished he was there in person.

Nodding again, Nef turned it on, and he heard it faintly in the background.

"Start using it," he growled.

Nef slowly pushed the toy inside, moaning softly with each thrust of her hand. Squeezing out some lube, Xander dropped the bottle onto the floor beside the bed and started stroking himself, watching Nef's face contort with pleasure.

"Are you thinking about fucking me?" He asked.

"Yes," Nef gasped, continuing to thrust the toy deeper.

"You shouldn't be," he said. Her hips bucked, and Xander groaned at the sight of her. He was almost jealous of the vibrator.

"What else should I be thinking of then?" Nef's eyes fluttered closed for a second.

"Being used, sweetheart. You're mine. I'm going to put you on your knees where you belong, and I'm going to make you suck like a good girl."

"Will you use the ropes?" Nef was undulating, and Xander picked up the pace of his strokes.

"Yes," he moaned. "I'm going to tie you up. You'll be so pretty, all marked and unable to move. I'll make you feel so good, Nef. I won't stop either. I'll make you beg for me, then beg for me to stop, and I'm going to make you forget everything but my name."

Nef moaned louder, thrust the toy faster, in and out, in and out. Sparks were running up Xander's spine and he forced himself to slow down, edging himself lightly. He didn't want to finish until Nef did.

"You like the idea of that, don't you sweetheart? You want to be bound and gagged, made to ride my cock until you can't take anymore?"

Xander could barely take it. He twisted his hand deftly, hard and rough, bringing himself back to the brink. He needed Nef so badly, needed to hold her, be inside her, be the one making her feel this way.

"Turn it all the way up," he demanded roughly.

Nef complied, throwing her arm up to cover her mouth and the scream that almost came out. She was lying back fully against her pillows now, so wet he could see her inner thighs glistening. Xander could imagine that he was there between her legs, licking up her centre, drunk on the taste of her.

"I need you to cum for me, sweetheart. Please honey. Need to see you." Xander was begging, and he didn't care.

He especially didn't care as Nef threw her head back and came with a muffled cry, legs shaking and back arching. God, she was gorgeous when she was coming for him. He wanted those legs shaking over his shoulders, wanted to feel her pussy quiver around him, drive him over the edge as he filled her up. White flashed in his vision as he came with a shout, spurting thick ropes of cum over his abdomen and chest.

When his breathing had finally gone back to normal and the ringing had left his ears, he looked up at his laptop. Nef was sitting up, a smug smile tugging at her lips. He smiled back, equally satisfied.

"Please tell me we're going to do that again," Xander dropped his head back with a sigh.

"Hell yeah."

Nef's tinkling laugh followed him into his dreams.

Tiye sat opposite Nef at the museum's cafe, nursing a large mug of coffee. It was quarter to seven in the morning, but the perks of being the owner and niece of the owner meant free pastries and a drink of choice before opening hours. In Nef's case, she was up to her second coffee. God knew she needed it in light of her plans for today.

"I've arranged for Oscar to meet you around the back. The storage room's been emptied so you have full use of it until the end of the exhibition." Tiye smiled over the rim of her mug. "I'm so proud of you, my little magpie."

Nef smiled proudly. Today, her curated pieces would arrive. The next several hours would be an anxious waiting game to make sure they came in one piece, followed by more anxiety as she directed her tradesmen to carry the pieces to the store room. It was imperative that they were stored correctly. She couldn't afford anything going wrong. Everything needed to be preserved, bubble wrapped, tagged, and ordered, to make sure that the set up would be as smooth as possible for when the hall was renovated.

"Aunty Tiye, what's better? Setting up the pieces before we put in the trees and lights, or after? I don't want anything to be knocked around."

"After." Tiye answered immediately. "Better to knock over a potted plant and sweep up the soil than to have to clean shards of a priceless artifact."

She made a good point. Scribbling in her notebook, Nef leafed over the binder she had spread out on the table before them. Most of the pieces had been designated a place, but she had yet to decide where to place Thuya's mask and the death scroll she had won in Xander's auction.

Her cheeks heated as she thought of Xander and last night. This is why she couldn't figure out where to put the pieces. She always got distracted.

"*Albee*," Tiye said in Egyptian. My heart. "Something else is on your mind. I may be old, but I too had a life once. You can talk to me, little magpie."

"I know, Aunty Tiye. There's nothing to tell, I promise."

Tiye's eyes narrowed. Crap. Lying to her aunt had never worked in the past. Tiye leant forward, and Nef took a huge gulp of coffee as though having her mouth full would deter her.

"There's a boy, isn't there." Tiye's eyes sparkled knowingly.

Swallowing loudly and immediately regretting it as her throat scalded, Nef gave a small nod of assent.

"Aha!" Tiye crowed. "Finally! You think you could hide it from me? Never. I know you, my little magpie."

This was why she rarely told Aunty Tiye about the men in her life. It had taken over a year with Gabriel before Tiye even suspected anything. Blushing, Nef spluttered unintelligibly as Tiye continued to speak.

"I won't push anymore, but I have to know. Are you happy?" Tiye's face had softened, become more serious.

Smiling, Nef nodded. "Very. We're taking things slow though."

"Good, good. Make sure you take things slow physically too — got to keep the mystery." Tiye winked and went back to her coffee, dropping the topic for now.

Beet-red and speechless, Nef went back to looking through her binder, not really seeing the pages. If only Tiye knew how much the mystery was solved. Shaking her head to clear her thoughts, Nef went back to planning her exhibit.

CHAPTER 25

God, Nef needed tonight. Another week had passed, a week of phone sex, constant texting, and hectic museum planning. Now, she stood with her girls, fully sober but on a sugar high at the club, surrounded by deep pulsing music that reverberated through her chest rhythmically.

Zara, Sophia, and Lilah were moving next to her, a blur of arms and swaying hips in a kaleidoscope of sparkling outfits. All of them were carefully balancing their cocktails in one hand (a pink lemonade for Nef), deftly murdering the dance floor in their six inch heels. Nef danced with them, her short, sparkly white dress flaring as she twirled in place, the scrappy corseted bodice hugging her curves.

Coming to this place was a tradition for them. Every time a major life event or achievement was approaching, they would start their night cooking together at one of their places, then move to the club to dance the nerves away. Not doing this before something important was bad luck. All of them swore by this method, the power of their friendship, and would plan months in advance to ensure they didn't have work the next day.

Tonight was for Nef. For her exhibition. It was exactly one month away now, and the renovations had finally been complete. A few patchwork jobs were left to do: blacking out the skylight, cleaning up the space properly, marking the floor for where each pillar and tree would be placed. Official invitations for opening night, not just the save the date ones Nef had made months ago, were ready and would be sent out by the end of the week. She was just waiting to hear about one more piece she wanted to display; the phone call could come any day now.

"Stop thinking so hard!" Lilah yelled over the music, taking her by her free hand. "You'll fuck up the ritual!"

Nef laughed and spun beneath Lilah's arm obediently. Zara joined her on her other side, blonde bob bouncing as she executed moves stolen from the seventies. Sophia was clearly tipsy, swaying to a completely imaginary beat.

"I'm going to grab another lemonade!" Nef loudly spoke into Lilah's ear. Nodding, Lilah proffered her the shared handbag so Nef could grab some cash. They all hated carrying bags to the club, so they rostered who took the group bag for the night. Grabbing enough for the drinks and a tip, Nef smacked a kiss onto Lilah's cheek, leaving a cherry red mark.

Giggling, Lilah blew a kiss back and danced away. Tapping Sophia on the shoulder, she gestured to her glass. She definitely wouldn't get her more alcohol, but god knew the woman could use several glasses of water right now. Soph shook her head though, instead grasping Zara's shoulders and trying to slow dance to Aqua's 'Barbie Girl'.

Smoothly dodging clubbers with varying degrees of spacial awareness, Nef made her way to the bar at the back of the underground joint. The same bartenders had been here for years, and knew exactly what to do when Nef smiled and handed over a handful of notes, with spare for the tip.

As Nef waited for her lemonade and Soph's water, she turned back to watch the crowd. It was more energetic, more wild than that charity ball she had been at with Xander, but watching everyone dance made her wish he was here with her. She wanted to be encircled in his arms, pressed against his solid chest. She wanted to dance for him, watch his eyes darken with desire until they left for her place in a rush, drunk on each other.

As though thinking of him brought him to life, a warm, deep male voice shook her from her daydream.

"I haven't seen you here before. What's your name?"

Turning to face the stranger, Nef took him in. Tall, with dark skin and short wavy black hair, he looked like a movie star with his blinding smile and muscled physique. Handsome, yes, but as Nef's eyes wandered over him, she found herself comparing him to Xander: not tall enough, not charming enough, not as well dressed. He lacked everything that made her attracted to Xander, and despite the truth, Nef immediately felt bad for thinking that of a man she didn't know. It wasn't her place to judge.

She smiled thinly, hoping he would take the hint and leave her alone. Nef was used to men hitting her up at clubs, but that didn't mean she wasn't tired of it. Funnily enough, this wasn't where she came to find a partner. And definitely no one night stands.

She thought back to Xander again. She loved that they were exclusive now, but she longed to make it official. To be able to tell people she was taken? Sure she was fine being single or not labelled, but it would be nice. She hadn't even told her friends about him yet (except Sophia of course). Did you tell friends when you were only exclusive?

"What's your name?" The man did not, apparently, get the hint.

Scanning the bar, Nef tried to see if her drinks were ready yet. Pink lemonade and a water bottle couldn't be taking this long. The man slid closer to her, a hand snaking out around her back to cage her in at the bar. Holding in a sigh, Nef knew the only way out was to fake and ditch.

Pasting a fake smile to her face, she was glad for the darkness of the club as it hid the murder in her eyes. Placing a hand firmly on his bicep to shove his arm off her, she crafted her lie.

"Oh! I didn't hear you over the music!" She made her voice a bit higher and more nasally than usual. "I'm here with someone though, sorry."

The man immediately drew back with an apology, and Nef's drinks finally arrived. Snatching them up, she stomped back to her friends, thankful her ploy had worked. Sometimes, men could be real pigs.

Reaching the circle of her chosen sisters, she shoved the water bottle into Sophia's hands and turned back to the centre of the group. Lilah was just hanging up on a call, slipping the phone back into the joint bag. Narrowing her eyes, Nef noticed it was her phone.

"Hey Lilah, did someone call me?"

Lilah scowled as she nodded. "I thought it might be about that hiero-, that hero, that history piece or whatever."

Smiling at Lilah's butchered slurs over 'hieroglyphics', Nef reached out a hand for her phone.

"I take it that wasn't them?" She unlocked her phone to check for the recent caller ID.

Xander's name appeared in red, and she grinned widely, ready to excuse herself to go call him back. But Lilah was still talking.

"Nah, just some asshole claiming to be dating you. I told him fat chance — you would have told us, and you wouldn't have been letting some guy hit on you at the club."

Nef froze. "What?!" She spluttered. "Hitting on me?"

Lilah gestured towards the bar. "You had a hand on his arm. Did he give you the ick or something?"

Groaning, Nef ran a hand through her curls. Of course Lilah didn't know you were faking, she told herself. Gripping her phone tightly, she excused herself and headed to the exit. Time for some damage control.

Xander was in bed trying not to make himself go prematurely bald. He had run his hands through his hair so many times in the last hour that it stuck up at weird angles, and not in a sexy 'I just woke up like this' kind of way.

He had just gotten off the phone with Nef. Gorgeous, smart, calm, devastating Nef, who had apologised profusely for Lilah and explained the situation.

On one hand, Xander loved that Nef had told him she'd never look at anyone else while in any kind of relationship — labelled or unlabelled. He trusted her, and knew how genuine she was, how loyalty and monogamy seemed buried in her DNA.

On the other hand, he was ready to strangle someone, mostly himself. Jealousy raged through his body, heightened after hearing Nef's rich sultry voice, hoarse from singing all night at the club.

Of course she had been hit on. He couldn't expect anything less for someone so utterly breathtaking, even though it was awful that women (and men) constantly received unwanted attention in those settings. He wished he could be there. It was possessive and irrational, but Xander wanted to make sure everyone saw him dancing with Nef, kissing her, taking her home. She was his, and he was hers. No one else's.

Unable to stand sitting in bed, Xander stalked into his living room. Here, he could pace between the open plan, modern, grey and metal kitchen, round wooden dining table, and living room with plush grey couches. Barefoot, he stormed over the deep red rugs placed over the wooden floors, almost knocking into a shelf of plants in the corner by the tv.

Why was he so frustrated? He had to figure this out or he'd never sleep. He had never been bothered by any of his past partners being hit on, but that had been because he knew it would only be a one night thing for him. Was this because he and Nef were exclusive? Did he feel like he should have done something more to prevent this? But the only thing he could do to truly show everyone they were taken was... was to declare them official.

Xander stood still in the middle of his apartment, balcony windows lit up by his outside lights. He waited for that familiar feeling of icy dread to sluice down his spine at the thought of a girlfriend.

It didn't come.

Did he... did he maybe want Nef to be his girlfriend? Xander stayed frozen, as though moving would bring back his usual terror when he thought of long term commitments again. When nothing happened, he kept going with his trail of thought.

He wanted to ask Nef to officially be his girlfriend. He wanted to be her boyfriend. He wanted to date her properly and take her out in public. He wanted her to tell all her friends about him, post photos of them together, show the world they belonged to each other alone.

Most of all, Xander thought he might want to tell Nef he was falling in love with her.

It was true, he thought slowly. He was falling in love. Maybe not yet fully there, but Nef consumed him. Her laughter, the way her nose scrunched when she didn't like something, the dirty jokes she quipped with a straight face, her red lips and lush curves and thoughtful commentary about the world. He wanted all of it.

Finally in control of his thoughts, Xander leaped back to his bed, rolling onto his back on top of the sheets. Now able to relax enough to sleep, he closed his eyes with a smile. He was going to ask Nef to be his girlfriend.

CHAPTER 26

It was almost lunch time, and Xander was hungry, horny, and fed up with his stupid meetings. Two of those things could be solved immediately; the meeting would end in five minutes, and once he got some food into him his employees would finally stop scattering as he rounded every corner.

The other issue, not so much. It was his own fault really. Four back to back meetings, each more boring than the last. Of course he had had to check his phone, make sure he wasn't missing anything *actually* important. Nef had sent him a selfie: red lips curved in a grin, curls tied up in a bun, showing off a store room filled with a myriad of scrolls, statues, ceramics, and more.

Xander's response had never made him feel so crudely male.

YOU GONNA DO WHAT I ASKED YOU TO THE OTHER NIGHT?

He doubted she had. Not only a few days ago, but his 'request' had been in the heat of the moment anyway. They had been getting hot and heavy over the phone, and Xander had bent to Nef's iron will and told her one of his fantasies — like their time in that shed at his excavation, he had said he wanted to see Nef get herself off in her store room at work. Something about the thought of her surrounded by her hard-won art, cheeks flushed and mouth slightly parted, coming undone while thinking of him made Xander crazy.

Not as crazy as Nef's response, which had come fifteen minutes later. It was a video, accompanied by a short "yes Sir". He had a pretty good idea what that video was of. And he had never been more grateful that he only lived three blocks away from his office.

Chairs started rolling back from the table, and Xander slumped back in his own, grateful to finally be able to get out of here. Grabbing his laptop, he waved goodbye to his colleagues and headed back to his place for the hour.

Xander was no longer hungry, horny, or fed up with meetings. Rather, he was tired and simultaneously bursting with nervous energy as he sat in front of Asim's desk, work hours having ended ages ago.

"So?" Xander's leg jerked quickly up and down under the table. "Does that sound romantic enough without also sounding desperate?"

Asim had a shit-eating grin on his face as he reread the handwritten scrawl Xander had come up with earlier that afternoon. It was supposed to be a draft of things to say when asking Nef to be his girlfriend, but as the silence dragged on Xander was more and more convinced it was about to become scrap paper.

Since when did asking someone to be official become this hard?

He remembered being in third grade, 'dating' one of his peers. That hadn't taken cringy drafts. Sighing, Xander kicked Asim's leg beneath the desk.

"Ach!" Asim mock yelled. "You monster. So rude to me when I'm slaving away here trying not to get you dumped for saying the wrong thing."

Xander's heart dropped. "You think she'll dump me?"

Relaxing back into his chair as Asim started cackling, Xander scowled. "Not funny, Asim. I really want to make this work with Nef. Only she can give me heart attacks, not you."

Asim put a hand to his heart and made an exaggerated sad face. "Why don't you just tell her that? Instead of all this flowery crap. I didn't even know you could write poetry."

"It's not poetry!" Xander felt himself blushing. Sure, he had consulted ChatGPT for some help. It had sounded great to him. But it wasn't poetry.

Laughing again, Asim handed the paper back to Xander, who promptly scrunched it up and chucked it vehemently into the nearby trashcan.

"Maybe I will just say that." Xander said miserably. He just wanted to wow Nef. Make her realise how much she had come to mean to him in such a short time. Make sure she said yes to a proper relationship, know she would be taken care of and cherished.

With a deep sigh, Asim rounded the table and placed a hand on Xander's shoulder. "I hate seeing you miserable. Honestly, just tell her what you've told me. She'll love it. And if she really wants a relationship with you, she won't really care what you said — just that you said it."

Finally cracking a smile, Xander grasped Asim's hand gratefully. "I'll ask her tomorrow. Right after the meeting."

"Sounds good, my friend. Keep me updated."

Breathing more easily, Xander said goodbye to Asim and headed back to his place. It was time to head to San Diego, his second home. And time to finally win over the girl of his dreams.

❖

The boxing bag thumped against the wall, rocking wildly from side to side as Nef deftly dodged. She was at the gym, and while swimming usually calmed her, today she wanted to hit something. She wanted to rage. Unfortunately, the bag was not putting up the fight the she wanted.

Hitting it again, Nef pounded away her frustration. She loved Aunty Tiye. The woman had practically raised her, become her mother and best friend all in one. But this morning, when Tiye had told her that the finalisation of the museum's sale would happen tomorrow, she had felt so much anger she could have sworn steam came out of her ears.

Despite having had months to come to terms with the end of the museum, Nef couldn't help but feel like this was personal. Whoever was purchasing her aunt's life's work had been some unseen evil entity. But tomorrow, they would become real. Some greedy landowner eager to create yet another set of ugly overpriced apartments. Nef doubted they would be sympathetic to the arts, not when San Diego already had so many other museums and attractions. Maybe this would become some fancy club that she would never be able to afford entry into.

Nef swung hard at the punching bag, then ducked as it swung right back. She almost wanted it to hit her, some sick masochistic part of her wanting to be punished for letting her aunt go through with this.

This museum was hers. It was special. Who had the right to come and take it from them? No one else understood how much it meant. Maybe Nef could work at another museum, but it just wouldn't be the same.

Maybe Sophia was right — therapy might help way more than boxing. Nef paused to drag a loose curl out of her eyes, considering Sophia's suggestion.

The only issue was that without the museum, Nef would have to pick up another job, possibly two, to help support both herself now that she wasn't working at the museum. She would be back to barely affording nights out, let alone therapy. And there was no way she would ask her aunt to help, no matter how much the museum sold for. Aunty Tiye had already done so much for her.

Nef debated calling Sophia to rant again, but that wouldn't be fair. Soph was out shopping for rings with Eliot, and Nef would never interrupt that for them. Maybe she could call Xander?

The thought was tempting, but it didn't sit quite right with Nef. She didn't want to dump her financial situation on him. It wasn't just too soon, but considering his financial situation, she didn't want to come across as whiny or as though he was asking for favours. As much as she was sure Xander would offer to help her just because he was a good, caring person, Nef wanted to earn her job and her money. And she never wanted to feel indebted to a man again, for anything.

They also weren't official yet. As great as being exclusive was, Nef had enough pride that she wasn't going to act like a girlfriend when she wasn't yet. Xander may not be all or nothing, but Nef certainly was.

Giving up on her one-sided fight, Nef unwrapped her hands, removed her earphones, and headed to the showers. Checking her phone, she scrolled through a bunch of new messages.

Sophia had texted her a bunch of photos of ring options. Smiling, Nef hearted the ones she thought would suit Soph most. Next were a bunch of messages from her aunt.

Nef hated fighting with her, and she knew none of this was really Aunty Tiye's fault. With a sigh, she detoured from the showers to a secluded bench in the back of the gym. Putting her earphones back in, she called her aunt.

Tiye picked up on the first ring. "Little Magpie! You know I never mean to upset you."

"I'm sorry, Aunty. I shouldn't have reacted that way. I know you're just doing what's best." Nef interrupted her quickly. She hated the guilt that always ate away at her chest whenever they fought.

"*Albee*, I must confess I haven't been entirely honest with you." Nef furrowed her brow. What did Tiye mean? They *never* lied to each other.

Tiye continued. "I misled you. You think you will need to find more work, support us both. I never said anything to suggest otherwise. I'm sorry. I hope you can forgive me. But I didn't want to say anything until it was confirmed."

"Say what, Aunty? Did the buyer offer more for the museum?" Nef's leg was bouncing up and down, butterflies surpassing her stomach and clogging in her throat.

Tiye laughed nervously. "Yes, but there is something else. I have a new job."

Nef froze. New job? That wasn't what she had been expecting. She was still trying to mentally connect the dots when Tiye spoke again.

"The university? They offered me a job, as a professor. They want me to take classes on management AND art curatorship. Me! Isn't that crazy?"

Glad she was already sitting, knee-wobbling relief, pride, and excitement swept through Nef.

"That's incredible!" Nef's voice was hoarse. Clearing her throat, she repeated herself. "I'm so proud of you. You deserve it. Students will be lucky to have you."

"Thank you, my magpie. I admit, it was you who inspired me. I'm excited to do something different. I'm just sorry it caused you so much stress."

"I have to ask though. Why did you need to sell the museum? Couldn't... couldn't I have taken over?"

"Oh, my darling. You are a gem. A true talent. Selling our museum was no reflection on you or your ability. I was being selfish — for the money, but also because I wanted this to be a new start for you as well.

You have been stuck here for so long, and I know you love it, but I think that's only because you never tried to make a home anywhere else. My deepest wish is for you to have the life I never had. That your mother never had."

Tears blurred Nef's vision. Her aunt was right. Maybe this was a good thing. Maybe she could let this go. Start fresh. If Aunty Tiye was brave enough to do this, then so was she.

Ending the phone call with emotional goodbyes and more "I'm proud of you's", Nef slumped back along the bench, still in disbelief. Her aunt was now a professor. Her aunt never doubted Nef's ability to take over. She hadn't realised how badly she had needed to hear that, hadn't recognised that that was the root of all her stress and anger. Laughter bubbled out of her slightly hysterically. She felt as light as a feather now.

Heading to the showers at last, Nef scrolled through her missed texts once more, stopping on her text chain with Xander.

I MISS YOU, it started. *FINALLY HEADING TO SAN DIEGO. NEED TO SEE YOU ASAP. MEET ME HERE TOMORROW AT 3PM?*

He had linked an address to her. Opening it, she laughed again. It was her museum! He must have googled her, found where she worked. It was sweet of him.

Nef spent the rest of the afternoon floating on cloud nine. She couldn't wait to see Xander again.

CHAPTER 27

Xander twisted his cufflinks in circles, the sleeves of his black shirt just slightly longer than his blazer. He was wearing a sacramento green suit today, his favourite colour. It was always luckier to wear his favourite suit for business meetings like this, especially when the one he had just finished was his first face to face business meeting since his ex.

Standing outside a humongous, elegant brick building three stories tall and an entire block wide, Xander felt a grin spread over his face as the morning sunk in. Everything had gone exactly according to plan. He had done it. Bought the museum.

What he'd do with it now, he had no idea, but the finalisation of the purchase meant he could finally relax, spend time with Nef, maybe show off the building and see if she had any ideas for what he should do with it. It also meant time in his childhood home — previously his grandfather's, then his mother's, renovated recently after she passed. It was still one of his favourite places to visit; it reminded him of her.

Checking his phone, Xander ignored Asim's message of congratulations, the notification from his bank that the transfer had gone through, and went straight to Nef's text chain to see if she had arrived yet. He had asked her to meet him at the museum out of convenience, but it seemed it was close to where she worked — he assumed she was at one of the smaller museums further towards her suburb, rather than in the central area.

It was 2:30pm, and Xander had plenty of time to relax before meeting Nef. Stomach growling, he made his way back into the museum and towards the cafe — now his cafe. Ordering a danish and coffee from the friendly waitstaff, he sat down at a table tucked in the corner by the doors. The coffee smelt amazing, but despite his hunger, Xander wasn't sure he could eat. The thought of seeing Nef again after almost a month was nerve-racking.

What if she didn't like him anymore? What if he was too late, and she had found someone else willing to give her everything he hadn't been?

Gulping at his coffee, Xander swore under his breath as he scalded his tongue. Think positive, he told himself. She'll show up and it'll be just as good as the first time.

Calming himself for the next few minutes by doom-scrolling through Instagram reels, Xander was distracted by a small commotion outside the cafe near the main entrance. A tiny woman, looking like a live-action Tinker-bell, was commandeering a troupe of men who were heaving large potted plants through the hall and towards the back of the lobby.

Watching amusedly, Xander thought the woman looked vaguely familiar, but he couldn't place from where. As the noise grew, the professor — and now ex-museum owner — entered the hall in a flourish of gauzy, multicoloured fabric.

She had dark brown skin leathery from age and decades in the sun, and thick corkscrew curls half wrapped in a bright coloured scarf. Geometric earrings swung from her lobes, and sharp black heels clicked on the marble and tile floor as she headed towards the blonde woman. When the woman turned her head, the gesture reminded Xander of Nef.

Checking his watch again for the time, Xander heard a second pair of heels rapidly click across the room. Looking up, he just had enough time to see the back of smart black heels, a pair of long, tan legs disappearing under a red pencil skirt, a crisp white blouse, and a head full of tumbling dark curls. The new-comer wove through the incoming crowd of visitors with ease, and Xander felt a cold, hard pit take root in his stomach.

Leaving his half drunk coffee cup behind, he slowly started to move towards the trio of women, now deep in conversation with one of the men who had been carrying the pot plants. The one with curly hair still had her back to him, and as he moved closer, the colourful professor turned sharply around and headed back towards her office, seemingly not noticing him.

The pit in Xander's stomach grew as the rest of the group dispersed. He was now halfway across the lobby, still a few meters away, when Nef turned around. Her red lips curved into a thrilled smile, and she did a cute little jump-hop into a power-walk towards him.

It seemed like this museum wasn't just convenient for her to meet at. It was where she worked.

Xander was going to throw up.

Slow down! Nef mentally yelled at herself as she tried not to launch herself towards Xander. It had only been a month, she needed to get a grip on herself. Grinning widely, she didn't give Xander a choice when she reached him, enveloping him in a tight hug.

Xander's arms rose around her immediately, his warm touch and hard body making her shudder slightly. He smelled delicious, and she couldn't get enough of him in his suit. It accentuated all the right places in all the right ways, and her fantasy of his hand wrapped around her throat while he fucked her, suit on and pants barely unzipped, flashed through her mind.

Blushing as she pulled away, she cupped Xander's cheek and lightly brushed a kiss to his mouth, avoiding smudging her lipstick.

"Hey, handsome," she whispered. Frowning, she finally took Xander in properly — he was staring at her shoulder, lips pressed tight and face pale. "You look like you've seen a ghost, Xander. Are you ok?"

Xander finally met her eyes and gave her a wan smile.

"I'm perfect, Nef," his voice was even better in person, deep and rich like wine — just as she had written in that note. "How could I not be when I'm finally next to you again?"

It was definitely a line, but Nef was more than happy to eat it up. "I just got off work — and I don't want you to see the exhibition until it's finished. Want to get out of here? I can't wait to hear about this new project of yours."

Xander's smile waned, and Nef winced imperceptibly. She knew face to face meetings were hard for him. Why did she bring it up? And right as they finally saw each other in person again. Jesus, she needed to stop overthinking every small action she made with this man.

"Getting out of here sounds good." Entwining their fingers together, Xander brought her hand to his mouth and pressed a kiss to the back of it. "Lets go back to mine?"

Flutters erupted in Nef's stomach. This felt important in a way, seeing his home. Intimate.

"I'd love that," she said. Heading out into the sunshine, Nef cheerily waved goodbye to Finn and Kelsie, today's front desk staff. Finn returned her wave enthusiastically, but Kelsie was more subtle, a concerned eyebrow and head nod towards Xander making her thoughts clear. Giving her a thumbs up behind her back, Nef focused again on the gorgeous man beside her.

Frowning again, Nef noticed he seemed stiffer, more reserved. She may not have known him for that long, but he had never acted like this while they were overseas. And definitely not while on the phone. In fact after last night, Nef was sure they might even be heading towards becoming official. She and Xander had talked for hours. He had asked her to be his plus one to another event in a month, and Nef had asked if he wanted to be hers to her exhibition. She had thought the call was a good sign.

Stop it, she scolded herself. It's not always about you. Maybe it's the meeting he had.

They reached the street and Xander hailed a cab, still holding Nef's hand tight. Peeking at his face again, Nef's resolve built. Running her free hand down his arm, Nef stepped in front of him and cupped his face again, forcing him to meet her gaze.

"Xander, honey," she said sternly. "What's wrong. You're never like this. You know I'm here for you no matter what right?"

It didn't matter how soon it was, it was true. Nef was in this a hundred and ten percent. Xander sighed and rolled his neck. Wrapping a hand around her waist, he pulled her in tight and kissed her deeply. It was a slow, languid kiss, one that made Nef's toes and core tingle in very pleasant ways. Every sweep of his tongue against hers made her forget what she had been asking, and when he pulled away at last, she continued leaning towards him with eyes closed hoping for just one more kiss.

His deep chuckle distracted her. Opening her eyes and giving him a mock pout, Nef felt thrilled that she had made him laugh.

"I've missed you," he murmured, pressing their foreheads together. "Sorry for being so out of it. I promise it's not you — that meeting just took a lot out of me."

Nodding, Nef tucked herself against his side as a cab finally pulled up to the curb. No other relationship, or even interaction, with a man had been so direct and reassuring. It wasn't her making him feel weird. Relaxing, Nef continued to run her hand up and down Xander's shoulder, sensing him leaning into her touch.

"Would a late lunch make you feel better?"

Xander finally smiled, and Nef felt as though she could bask forever in the glow she felt when he directed it at her.

"I'll cook," he said.

CHAPTER 28

As they walked into his town house, Xander tried to see it from Nef's perspective. A long but thin whitewashed building, the entryway led straight to a hallway lined with a multicolour rug and some tall fronds. A staircase to their right led up to two bedrooms — now his master bedroom and ensuite, and a small office. Leading her through the hall and past the small bathroom, they entered into a cozy but spacious open plan area, with the kitchen directly to their right, separated from plush red couches and colourful pillows by an island and small round dining table.

Knowing Nef was likely taking everything in with her curator's eye, Xander was grateful for the various paintings along the wall, interspersed with framed photos of him as a kid with his mom.

Hmm. Maybe he didn't want those photos up on display just yet.

Nef was slowly moving through the house, taking everything in with wide eyes. Her curiosity was endearing — she stopped for a few seconds as she passed each painting, roving over the details with wide eyes.

Seeing her barefoot in his childhood home soothed something inside Xander he hadn't realised was jagged. She just fit, somehow.

He watched her as hungrily as she watched the art. Despite knowing now that he had bought her aunt's museum — something he hadn't even had time to grapple with yet — the effect she had on him hadn't changed at all.

She padded softly towards him, hips swaying tantalisingly in that tight red skirt, making his cock stand stiffly to attention. Red was his new favourite colour.

Nef's eyes darted to his crotch, her sensuous mouth curving wickedly into a knowing smile.

"I know we said food first, but there's something else I want to eat right now," she smirked.

Laughing, Xander crossed the rest of the room to meet her, slightly pressing her back against the kitchen island. "I hope you don't use that line on every man."

"Too cheesy?" The window behind her looked out on the side garden, a narrow strip of concrete bordered by vines of Jasmine and passionfruit buds. Nef tilted her chin up to look him in the eye, her rich brown gaze dazzling in the afternoon sunlight.

"Cheesy, yes. But it's still working. May I give you a tour of the bedroom?"

Taking her hand, he led her up the stairs and into another narrow hall, smaller than the last. Opposite the stairs was a small window with a tiny bookshelf underneath, and two doors stood down the hall on their left.

Xander pulled Nef into the first door, which opened into a cozy, minimalist bedroom. On the wall opposite them was a small white chest of draws that sat underneath another window. A queen-sized bed covered in a thick white doona and several, equally plush, pillows sat against the wall to their right. A large mirror was hung on the wall opposite the bed, and a small bedside table closest to the entry had a single old fashioned lamp. In the left corner, another door led to the ensuite.

Nef shot him a glance before walking into the small space, heading straight to the window.

"You grew up here?" Nef asked.

"Yep. The ensuite is new. It used to be two bedrooms — one for me and my mom, because my grandfather never lived with us. He just owned the place."

Wrestling with a scowl, Xander tried not to think too hard about his grandfather. He was already in a tumultuous emotional position, and Nef didn't deserve to have to put up with that.

As though sensing his turmoil, Nef turned back towards him and ran her hand up his arm soothingly.

"That must have been hard, Xander," she murmured.

Nodding tiredly, he leant into her touch. She was so warm, so soft. He wanted to pull her into bed and take turns spooning each other, spend hours playing with her hair and letting her listen to him rant about his childhood.

Nef's other hand starting running up his other arm, and she slowly wrapped her hands around his neck, pressing her body tightly to his. Biting back a groan at the feel of her generous chest against his, Xander immediately grabbed her waist and pulled her as close as possible.

Thoughts of cuddling were quickly replaced with thoughts of Nef in various lewd positions, that pretty red mouth being put to use.

Reaching down to cup her ass, Xander nuzzled her neck before biting her ear lobe, teeth dragging lightly back down the curve of her neck. He grinned to himself as she shuddered beneath him, hands flying up to grip his hair as he slowly drew circles on the back of her upper thigh. Lifting her skirt higher and higher, Xander growled as he felt the bare skin of her ass.

"No panties?" His voice was low and foreign to him.

Nef smiled smugly, eyes hooded with lust. "All for you. Sir," she added.

"Such a good girl for me," Xander crooned. He captured her mouth in a bruising kiss, pulling away too soon and leaving them both panting. His hands were still edging her skirt higher, and it was starting to bunch around her waist, pulling the hem of her white blouse with it.

"I want everything off. Now."

Nef responded to his order enthusiastically, practically ripping at her buttons and skirt zipper. Her clothes were in a neat pile on the floor in under a minute, and Xander enjoyed tracking the path of her lacy cream bra as she dropped it on the very top.

Finally. Nef stood in front of him, bathed in sunlight. She looked... he didn't have the words. Breathtaking. Like a goddess. Everything about her made him want to drop to his knees and please her in the only ways he knew how.

Watching her standing there, waiting for his next order, Xander realised he could do exactly that.

"On the bed."

Nef immediately crawled onto the covers and lay down on her back, propping herself up on an elbow to watch him. Not bothering with his own clothes yet, Xander gripped her ankles and dragged her to the edge of the bed, spreading her legs open so he stood between them.

Ignoring Nef's small gasp of surprise, Xander did what he had wanted to do for the past month. He dropped to his knees, gripped her inner thighs to keep her open, and started to feast.

Xander didn't know how long had passed, but Nef's moans were getting louder and breathier; he knew she was close. Holding back a smile he stopped his ministrations, hovering teasingly above her centre.

Nef tried to sit up to see what was happening, but he stopped her with a firm hand on her abdomen. Clicking his tongue, he frowned at her.

"Don't move. Tell me what you want." Nef let out a moan.

"Please," she begged. "Please, you know what I want."

"I want you to say it."

Nef whimpered and shifted her hips higher, closer to his mouth. "Please..."

"Please what?" Xander betrayed no amusement on his face, no mercy. God, he loved it when Nef begged. Loved knowing he was the one making her this wet, this turned on. Without warning, he dipped his head and licked up her core in one long stroke.

"Ah!" Nef gasped. "Please, please Xander."

Xander gave another long, slow lick, savouring the taste of her, the feel of her as she quivered beneath him. Then he pressed an open mouthed kiss to her inner thigh, to the sensitive nub at the top of her sex.

"Please what?" He said again. "You know I don't like to repeat myself, sweetheart."

"Please... eat my pussy," red flooded Nef's cheeks, but Xander only chuckled lightly. And then his mouth was on her, licking and sucking, revelling in the way Nef undulated and gripped his hair, pulling him to where she felt best.

"God, Xander," Nef's moans were getting louder again, and Xander let out a moan of his own at the sound of his name on her lips. He didn't think he would ever get used to it.

Shifting slightly, he added first one finger, then two. Nef had moved from his hair to his arm, tightly gripping the hand that he had locked over her stomach to keep her in place. Her nails raked lightly at his skin as he pumped his fingers into her, over and over again.

Xander was unrelenting. Adding a third finger, he lightly scraped his teeth over that sensitive nub, soothing it with a flick of his tongue. Nef came with a garbled cry, a mix of sobs and his name, the sound shooting straight to his aching cock which had slowly started leaking pre-cum.

"Xander, please, please that's enough," she panted. But Xander wasn't done yet. He kept going, licking her through her orgasm, an iron grip on her hips keeping Nef spread for him even as she struggled to shift away.

"Please Xander," Nef nearly sobbed from the over-stimulation. "I can't come again."

Challenge: accepted. With one last, longing lick, Xander looked up from where he kneeled, stubble covered in her arousal. Loosening the buckle of his belt, he started tugging off his clothes to give Nef a short reprieve.

"You can go again," he nearly growled. "Because I say so."

The subtle lifting of Nef's hips told Xander he was right. Not taking his eyes of hers, he crawled onto the bed on top of her, sparks of pleasure tingling in his veins as he brushed against her damp thighs. Reaching for the bedside draw, he swore as he came up empty handed.

"Nef, I don't have condoms here." How could he have been so stupid? He sat up on his knees, pulling away from her. "I'm so sorry honey. We can go to the pharmacy after lunch?"

Nef stopped him with a hand on his chest. "I'm clean. And I'm on the IUD."

Xander could have married her then and there. "I'm also clean. But are you sure?"

Nef nodded eagerly, stroking his cock and lining him up with her pussy. "I'm sure."

Suddenly, Nef tensed up.

"What is it, sweetheart?"

Nef chewed on her bottom lip, looking away from his gaze. "Sorry, it's just…It's just been a while… I forgot how big you are."

Smirking, Xander leant down and pressed a gentle kiss to the corner of her mouth. Another one to the other corner. She was so cute, thinking that that would be an issue. Or that that would stop him if it was. He finally pressed his lips fully to hers, and as she opened for him, her tongue meeting him stroke for stroke, he pressed slowly inside her.

They both groaned at the movement, at the smooth slide of him deep, deeper into her, wet from her orgasm and arousal. Xander swore this was what heaven felt like — Nef, warm and tight and perfect beneath him. He had thought he would ruin her, but maybe it would be the other way around.

Suddenly, pleasure gave way to guilt and Xander's slow thrusts stuttered. He had ruined her, and she didn't even know it yet. He had bought her aunt's museum, the one she had raved about and shared with him and talked about how special it was to her. The one where she was holding her first solo exhibition, with artifacts she had won in his auction. How could he be fucking her like this when he knew that once she found out what he'd done, it would break her heart?

Nef's legs wrapped around his hips, drawing him closer.

"Don't stop, honey," she gasped. "Please, I can't take your teasing anymore!"

God, he couldn't stop now. Xander felt like he was being torn in half, pleasure and guilt mixing through his blood like a poisonous soup. Trying to push his anguish at what he had done to the side, he started thrusting again. Hard, fast thrusts, a punishment for them both, though he couldn't discern why yet.

"Look at you," Xander whispered into her ear. "My perfect girl, so warm and tight for me."

Nef's moans filled the room, joined by Xander's harsher grunts as he thrusted even harder.

"You feel," she panted between thrusts, "so fucking good."

Groaning, Xander moved onto his knees and lifted one of Nef's legs over his shoulder, the deeper angle making her cry out again.

"Next time," he said, "I'm going to bend you over in front of the mirror, and take you like that. I want to see your face as you watch me fuck you, as you struggle to stand from how much pleasure you're feeling."

Moving her hips in time with his, Nef whimpered in approval. "Next time, I want to try toys. I want to use a vibrator so I can cum all over your cock while you fill me up."

Fuck, that did it.

Xander bucked against her, slamming to a stop as his orgasm rushed through him. Nef was trembling, her own orgasm crashing over her just as suddenly. Slowly pulling out, he lowered himself half on top of her, one arm wrapping protectively over her chest.

"Wow," Nef flopped closer to him, nuzzling her nose into the crook of his neck. She looked so happy, so peaceful. No clue that he had just betrayed her so thoroughly, no matter the fact that he didn't know until the deal was done.

Making a vague noise of assent, the guilt crashed over Xander again with a renewed vigour. He had no idea how to tell her, and frankly, he didn't want to. What they had was special, he could feel it. He didn't want to be the one to destroy it, but a sick feeling in his stomach told him he already had.

CHAPTER 29

Several hours (and several rounds) later, Nef was busy admiring Xander's muscled arms as he deftly served her a steaming plate of home-made fettuccini. Watching him in the kitchen was something she could totally get used to, especially when he was cooking for her, and with such a sexy look of concentration on his face the whole time.

He glanced up from where he was ladling a mushroom sauce over his own plate, grinning at her. Nef's smile back was wide, but not entirely genuine.

Something was off.

She knew Xander had told her not to worry, but she also trusted her gut. And right now her gut said that something didn't feel right. Gulping down her glass of water to distract herself, Nef crossed and uncrossed her legs, trying to think about how to bring it up again without being pushy.

"What does your schedule look like, sweetheart? I need to know when to plan our dates."

Whiplash. Was something off? That didn't sound like a troubled man. But then again, she had dated a troubled man for years without realising. Never again.

"I'm busy 8-4 most days of the week, but evening's I'm usually free?"

"Perfect." Xander flashed her another smile and Nef felt herself go a bit weak in the knees. He really was gorgeous. She still couldn't believe she was in his childhood kitchen, eating food he had made for her. "Can I book you tomorrow for dinner? 7pm?"

"One sec let me check," Nef pulled up her Google calendar and cursed softly. "Sorry Xander, I'm with my aunt tomorrow night. Hang on —"

Pausing, Nef typed out a quick message to her aunt. Not even thirty seconds later, and Aunty Tiye had responded. Xander watched her intently the whole time, his piercing gaze making Nef's whole body tingle pleasantly.

"Ok! If you'd like — and so fine if it's too soon — you're welcome to join us for dinner?"

Nef knew she wore her heart on her sleeve, so she tried her best to stop her face from falling as Xander hesitated.

"I don't want to intrude," he held up a hand placatingly. "It's your time with your family, so I won't interrupt."

"You're not intruding at all!" God, he was so sweet. Nef loved him even more for being so respectful of her time with her aunt. Fuck. Loved? Nope. Tucking that thought away in the deep recess of her mind, Nef decided to not make her head hurt today. Future problem for a future time.

"Please come, Xander. I'd love to have you there."

When he hesitated again, Nef decided to play dirty. Hopping off her stool she rounded the island and wrapped her hands around Xander's waist. Kissing his neck gently, she made sure to lick and suck in the way she knew made him lose control.

"Please come, Xander," she whispered. "It would mean a lot to me."

Sure enough, his hands flexed on her hips, hard enough to bruise. Pulling her flush against his powerful body, he sighed then nodded, pressing his forehead to hers.

"Only for you, sweetheart."

He leaned down to kiss her, and Nef let him swallow her triumphant grin.

***

The smell of Aunty Tiye's cooking wafted through the small apartment, and her stomach rolled with a mix of nerves and hunger. Xander was supposed to arrive in less than ten minutes.

Smoothing down her blue satin skirt, Nef paced hurriedly towards the kitchen. Tiye was flitting between the stove and oven, curls held back from her face with a rainbow headband. A cookbook lay open on the wooden dining table, already set for three with their best cutlery.

Their home was small, cozy. Had been the same before the museum gained success, and would stay the same after it was sold. No amount of money could replace the comfort they both felt here, where they both had slowly healed after Cleo (naturally short for Cleopatra) fell into her coma.

Nef hoped Xander liked it. Suddenly, she couldn't help but feel as though everything she was, all she had to offer, was inadequate for him. She knew otherwise, but the fear, like all her other niggling doubts, lodged in the back of her mind as she chewed on her bottom lip.

Tutting, Tiye flapped her hand at Nef without turning around from the stove. "You'll ruin your lipstick, little Magpie."

"You're not even looking at me!" Nef squawked.

"I don't need to," Tiye smirked as she turned around. Proffering her a spoon, Nef accepted and leant forward to test if the couscous was ready. Humming her appreciation, Nef reached for another spoonful but was again thwarted by her aunt slapping her hand away lightly.

Huffing amusedly, Nef gave up and headed back to the living groom, aiming to collapse onto the couch and try read a bit to calm her nerves. Before she could though, the intercom buzzed. Skidding to the phone by the door, her aunt beat her to it. Voice muffled, Tiye buzzed Xander up.

Shuffling footsteps announced Tiye walking up behind Nef, ready to greet their guest. Turning to face her, Nef smiled at her red 'kiss the cook' apron, a Mothers Day gift from years ago.

"Do I get to know anything other than his first name now?" Tiye nudged her softly between the ribs with an elbow.

Nef made a vague noise. "You'll like him, Aunty."

"Oh, I don't doubt that I'd like any man who treats you right. You tell this young man of yours that he's welcome to send me perfume anytime."

Nef laughed nervously as Tiye winked at her. A sharp knock sounded at the door, and Nef's stomach leapt.

"I think you can tell him yourself," Nef grinned.

His collar was choking him. Xander had debated the whole day how he could cancel dinner without looking like a complete coward — and an asshole. He still hadn't told Nef about the museum, and the more time that passed, the worse he felt.

To top everything off, Xander knew that the second the door opened, Professor Perez would recognise him instantly and the whole night would be ruined.

Groaning loudly in frustration and self-loathing, Xander went to tug on his hair before resisting. He had already gotten ready, and if he was going to destroy what he had thought was his first healthy, hopefully long term relationship, he wanted to at least look like he had some dignity left.

He may be an asshole, but he kept his promises. And he had promised Nef he would come tonight.

Sighing, he grabbed his keys and headed off to his inevitable doom.

***

The car ride over was too fast and too slow. Parking outside Nef's complex, Xander buzzed the intercom and was quickly let in by her aunt. Hopefully, Professor Perez hadn't recognised his voice and told Nef already. He at least wanted to break the news to her himself, in person.

Stomach twisting, he reached her door and knocked sharply. Drumming his fingers against his thigh, his mouth went dry as he heard voices behind the door go silent, and a few footsteps towards him. The door swung open.

Xander cursed every god he knew of.

Nef looked radiant, her light blue skirt making her tanned olive skin glow. Her curls made a voluminous halo down her back, and her aunt looked equally as regal standing behind her. He didn't know if he should laugh or wince at that apron.

Wincing won out, as his eyes bounced between Nef's excited smile and the professor's jaw dropped expression.

Pulling out a bouquet of roses from behind his back, he plastered a smile on his face and prayed his voice didn't squeak.

"For you, Mrs Garcia," he held out the flowers, his metaphorical white flag for Nef's aunt.

Please don't say anything, please, he mentally chanted. Jaw protesting at how hard he was clenching his teeth, the silence stretched out for a beat too long.

A gracious smile spread across Tiye's face, and she reached out to accept the roses.

"Alexander, thank you. It's so nice to finally meet the man Nef has told me so little about!" Tiye shot a pointed glance at Nef, who blushed faintly. "Please, come in! And you can call me Tiye."

Xander's knees wobbled with relief and guilt. She was playing along — for now. "Nice to meet you, Tiye. You can call me Xander."

As Tiye walked ahead down the hall, Xander wrapped an arm around Nef's waist and pulled her into a deep kiss. He savoured the taste and feel of her, the way she sighed into his mouth and dragged her nails briefly along his scalp.

This could be their last kiss.

The thought shuddered through him, tightening his stomach into coils. Xander pulled away reluctantly, coils turning to lead as Nef started leading him to the kitchen, pointing out the main rooms as they went. Tonight was no doubt about to become a train wreck.

Breathing in deeply, Xander nodded along absently to Nef's animated tour. They finally entered the kitchen, and Xander calmed his thoughts enough to take in the small but modern room with a single window on the far wall and a four-person table set for three.

Tiye had already placed his roses in a vase in the centre of the table. The room smelled incredible. Xander could barely place half the spices, and his stomach growled loudly.

Nef chuckled. "I'm glad you're hungry. Aunty Tiye's food is so good you'll be rolling out of here!"

Smiling weakly, Xander murmured his agreement. He was useless right now. The guilt was eating him alive.

"Nef, sweetheart, can I talk to you for a sec?" Xander leaned down to speak quietly in her ear, the scent of her perfume calming him slightly. "Privately?"

"Oh! Sure thing. Let's go to the living room?" Nef placed a hand on his arm, brows furrowed. "Is everything ok?"

"No. Yes. I —"

"Dinner's ready! Sit, sit, please." Tiye swept over from the stove, glasses fogged from the heat of the dishes. Ushering them to the table, Xander had no choice but to match Nef's sympathetic smile as she mouthed 'later' and took her place in the middle seat.

Sitting opposite Tiye, Xander felt his palms start to sweat as she watched him silently, a subtle puzzled frown tugging at the corners of her mouth. She knew. She definitely knew he hadn't told Nef.

He felt like the world's biggest asshole. He shouldn't have come tonight. He didn't deserve to be here.

Oblivious to the rising tension, Nef generously loaded his plate with piles of succulent kebabs, kofta, couscous, and dips. She was talking, but the blood rushing through his ears drowned her out.

Suddenly, Tiye sat up straighter, and opened her mouth to speak.

CHAPTER 30

Nef watched with fading amusement as Xander visibly took a few seconds to comprehend her aunt's question. Something was definitely off. Gently squeezing his knee under the table, Nef repeated Tiye's question.

"Xander, honey, could you please pass the kofta?"

Bewildered, he passed over the plate of succulent meat, colour slowly returning to his face. They all tucked into their meals, but the flavour was lost to Nef as worst-case scenarios flooded through her head.

What on earth was going on with Xander?

Stilted conversation finally started flowing, as Tiye engaged Xander in a conversation about his latest excavation and upcoming auctions. Pushing around the couscous on her plate, Nef watched them silently, nodding when appropriate.

Something was up. Nef needed to know what it was, because it was starting to make her jittery. Leg bouncing under the table, she debated how best to bring it up — after dinner, of course, when Aunty Tiye wasn't there to witness.

A slow caress along her leg drew her out of her thoughts. Xander was still talking with Tiye, now more animated and visibly relaxed. As he continued gesturing with his fork, his other hand drew soothing circles down her thigh, around her knee, until Nef finally relaxed her legs and stopped shaking. Now his turn to gently squeeze her knee, Xander shot her a calming smile before turning back to her aunt.

This man was making her crazy. Crazy, and a little bit in love.

That decided it. Nef straightened up and dipped her kebab generously into some tzatziki. She loved this man. Maybe people would think it was too soon, but something in her gut told her that she was right to feel this way. Xander made her feel safe, understood, sexy, cared for. It didn't matter to her if someone else could do the same, she had chosen Xander. And no matter what was going on with him right now, what worst case scenario might be happening (except for cheating, Nef did like to think she had standards), she would stick with him through it all.

Determination coursing through her, Nef finally joined the conversation. It was time to show Xander how much he meant to her.

***

Her smile was so wide it hurt her cheeks. Xander was in her bedroom. Xander was in her bedroom, looking literally edible. He was standing at her desk, eyes roving over the various blueprints she had sticky-taped to the wall while planning her exhibition.

It was a great view, Nef thought. Of him, not the blueprints. With his collared shirt tucked into his slacks, she could see the outline of his bubble butt from her position on her bed. She kind of wanted to bite it.

Unfortunately, it wasn't the right time for her head to be in the gutter. Aunty Tiye had kicked them out of the kitchen so she could finalise dessert, and the pair had practically rolled to her room, sleepy and stuffed.

"Your exhibition is going to be amazing, Nef. The plans look incredible." Xander looked back at her, a relaxed grin on his face tugging at her heart strings.

Nef blushed, smile somehow widening further. "Thanks, Xander. I can't wait for you to see it."

Xander looked away from her and dragged a hand through his hair. Nef liked that dishevelled look on him. Sitting up onto her knees, Nef held out a hand towards Xander, ready to pull him down onto the bed with her.

"Honey, I wanted to talk to you," she started nervously.

Xander's head whipped around, and Nef nearly jumped. Her heart was beating a hundred miles an hour.

"It's nothing bad!" She rushed on. Xander looked like a deer in headlights, and she wanted to calm him, hold him. "I just wanted to talk about us. About where we're heading."

Nef watched Xander closely. His throat bobbed, and he wasn't looking at her again. A chill spread through Nef's chest. His current jumpiness was completely at odds with his earlier affectionate behaviour. God she was sick of these mixed signals. She cleared her throat, bolstering herself to finally tell Xander how she felt, what she wanted.

"I need to tell you about my new project." Xander's voice was rough and low.

A breath escaped Nef in a rush. His project? Maybe his meeting hadn't gone well. An uncomfortable twist of guilt and relief pooled in her stomach. As bad as it was, she'd rather Xander's behaviour be because of his work and not because of her. Chewing on her bottom lip, Nef waited silently for Xander to continue.

"I…" he trailed off, throwing a glance towards her before continuing to survey the wooden floorboards. With an air of exhaustion, he slumped down on the edge of the bed, and took her hand.

"I told you I was buying a piece of land right?"

Nef nodded slowly.

"Well, I wasn't entirely honest."

Her stomach dropped. "Xander, whatever happened with your project, I'm here for you. Ok?"

Xander shook his head and his grip on her hand turned tighter. She squeezed back, trying to pour her support and love into her touch.

"It wasn't just the land. It was a museum. I didn't tell you what my plans were because, well, I didn't want to jinx it, and... I also had no idea that it was your museum."

Blood rushed through her ears like a phantom scream.

Your museum. Her museum. Please don't keep going, she silently pleaded; please don't say what I think you're going to.

"I'm so sorry Nef," he was still talking, holding her hand to his chest and finally looking at her, devastation written on his gorgeous face. "If I had known, I... I... I'm so sorry. I know how much the museum meant to you, and I can't believe I never connected the dots. The last thing I wanted to do was hurt you."

Xander — her Xander, who she trusted and ranted to and thought she loved — was saying that *he* had bought her aunt's museum. Xander was the anonymous buyer.

All those times she had ranted to him and told him how important this museum was, how upset she was about this being her first and final solo exhibit at a place that meant the world to her, meant nothing.

"How long have you known?" Nef's voice was icy calm, shocking even herself.

Xander had the decency to look ashamed. "Since yesterday morning. I finalised the purchase with Tiye, and then I saw you guys together. That's when I realised. Nef—"

"If you had known, would it have changed anything?" Nef didn't realise how badly she needed to know his answer until he gave it.

"I told you, Nef." Xander's anguished expression made her heart hurt even more. "I always chose what I love most. My work has always come first. But now it's different! I wanted to tell you —"

Nef held up a hand. "I'm going to need time to process this. And I want to be very clear: I get that you didn't know. Fine. But you found out yesterday, spent the day and night with me, came to dinner at my place, talked to my aunt *who you already knew*, and didn't say anything until now?"

Her voice had risen, reverberating through the bedroom. The fury must have been evident on her face, because Xander had let go of her hand and was now gripping her doona instead, apologising over and over again.

Nef heard nothing but the sound of her own heart shattering.

A small voice in the back of her head told her this wasn't the worst thing in the world. That they could come back from this, that Xander hadn't known and the museum was sold regardless of who the buyer was. But a louder voice was rampaging across her consciousness, demanding that she scream, cry. Anything to ease the pain she was now feeling knowing that Xander had known and kept this from her, that he had said he would always choose work first. That Aunty Tiye had played along tonight.

"I need you to leave," Nef spoke softly. "I need you to go home, and not contact me until I contact you. I need to process this, and then we can talk."

"Anything," Xander breathed. "I'll do anything you ask. I can't lose you."

Nef turned away from him, tears blurring her vision. "Please leave, Xander. I want to talk to you. But not now."

She didn't look as he got off the bed. She didn't look as he brushed a kiss to the top of her head, the small touch apology and sadness and hope all in one. She didn't look as he left her bedroom, as the front door closed behind him. And she didn't look as she curved in on herself, tears finally escaping her in sobbing heaves.

CHAPTER 31

The next morning was fucking agony. Xander was sleep deprived, coffee deprived, and Nef deprived. The uncertainty of when she would contact him was already almost breaking him, and it hadn't even been twenty four hours.

He was ready to grovel. Get on his knees and beg. Anything to make sure her face never looked as shocked and hurt and betrayed as it did last night.

Xander was also confused. Did last night mean they had broken up? Surely not. Nef had said she wanted to talk to him. He had grabbed onto her words like a drowning man's lifeline. Even if she wanted to end things now — and he couldn't blame her if she did — at least he'd see her one more time. The only question was when.

Xander spent the day miserable, moping around his townhouse and rewatching 'Legally Blonde' — one and two. Every few seconds he checked his phone. He turned into an unrecognisable couch-gremlin, in grey sweatpants and an old Giants shirt, auburn hair loose around his shoulders, mugs of half drunk cold tea littered around the coffee table between two boxes of pizza and a garlic bread.

He hadn't even been this bad with Elissa.

When the living room was finally lit up with only the light of the blaring TV, Xander forced himself to clean up and eat something more substantial. Choking down an omelet made with leftover groceries, he dragged himself to a shower and then to bed.

Still no contact from Nef.

The day after, Xander stayed in bed all morning, contemplating how he had so royally screwed up. He had been so happy with Nef and hadn't even realised. If she had waited, hadn't interrupted him the other night, he would have told her that he thought he was falling for her and wanted them to be official.

The idea that he might never get that chance made Xander sick.

On the third day, Xander was ready to be put out of his misery. In a ten minute phone call, Asim managed to somehow piss him off, offer commiserations, and give

Xander the week off from work, citing reasons as 'heartbroken simp'.

Now, Xander was lounging on the couch in nothing but forest green plaid pyjama pants, eating ice cream for breakfast straight from the tub. He finally got why girls always did this in movies, and man, was he on board with it. He only felt awful, compared to yesterday when he felt absolutely terribly awful.

It's the small wins in life.

Licking off a spoonful of mint chocolate ice cream (the superior flavour and a hill he was willing to die on), Xander wondered if Nef was doing the same thing he was. Shaking his head, he tried to focus on the reality TV show playing. Thinking of Nef was painful. He both missed her and was also a little bit mad that she hadn't contacted him yet. He hadn't told anyone else what was happening — aside from his therapist, who he had another appointment with next weekend.

Groaning, he dropped his head back on the pillows and abandoned the ice cream on the low table in front of him. He wanted to bury himself in hot sand and forget the last few months entirely.

A loud knock broke Xander out of what had become his daily morning pity party. Ignoring his shirt, he padded softly to the entrance where he could make out the shape of Nef's figure behind the frosted stained glass door.

Stopping just in front of the glass, Xander paused. He wanted to open it so badly. But what if she was just here to break things off officially?

Don't be a coward, he told himself silently. Maybe things will be ok.

Ignoring the tremors in his hands, Xander opened the door. It was only when Nef's face — for once void of any lipstick — dipped straight to his chest did he remember he was only wearing pyjama pants. Thanking the universe for making him remember to shower earlier, Xander crossed his arms self consciously and leant between the door and the doorframe.

"Hey," his voice didn't squeak, thank god.

"Hey," Nef said back, voice small. She looked tired, almost as though she had been crying recently. For a second, Xander was selfishly glad she wasn't doing great, but that thought was quickly overrun by guilt and disgust that he had made her feel this way. She was probably more upset that he had bought her museum than the fact that they had fought.

"Can I come in?" Nef was still standing outside, shifting from foot to foot. It was a hot day, but Nef was wearing a long orange skirt and a heavy-looking cream collared blouse.

Sighing, Xander stood aside to let her enter. Like he would ever shut Nef out of his life, even if she was here to break his heart.

The pair walked silently into the living space, and Xander cringed as he watched Nef take in his nest of blankets on the couch, the condensation dripping off the ice cream tub on the coffee table. He didn't blame her when she smoothly detoured to the kitchen island instead, perching delicately on a stool as he rounded the other side of the island opposite her. They stared at each other, the silence loud.

Clearing his throat, Xander looked away first. "What can I do for you, Nef?"

She fidgeted on her seat, stalling. Xander was ready to burst.

"I wanted to tell you in person," Nef blurted suddenly. "I want to try work through this with you, but I don't... I just don't think I feel the same way anymore. I don't know if I ever will, but I want to try."

"Try to work through this? What do you mean?" Xander's voice sounded as hollow as he felt at Nef's revelation. He really had fucked up.

"I mean... let's give this a few months and see how it goes? If I still feel like this at the end, then..." Nef trailed off softly. Xander wanted to look at her, but everything felt so heavy, so weighed down.

Staring at the now-fascinating speckles of colour flecking the island's stone top, Xander tried to make his thoughts coherent.

"I'm sorry, Nef. I want to try work through this too, but I don't want to give our relationship a deadline. Have you thought about how miserable that will be? You'll spend every moment comparing your feelings for me from before this to now, and I'll spend every moment imagining you doing that and deciding that you don't want me anymore. That isn't fair, to either of us. I'd rather just end things now than prolong it for a few months until you get to call things off again."

Xander was breathing heavily, gripping the edge of the island with white knuckles. He hadn't realised how upset Nef's idea had made him. Or how awful it would feel to suggest they break up out loud.

Nef had shrunk back into her seat, head bowed. Xander hated the pain in her voice, hated seeing her eyes filled with tears when she spoke again.

"I'm so sorry Xander. I just don't know if I'll feel the same way again. You lied to me. That's a deal breaker. And you lied about something that you *knew* was important to me."

Every word was a punch to the gut. Yes, he hated Nef's deadline idea, but what if there was something else they could do to salvage this? He had told her he'd do anything.

"Nef..." Xander rounded the island towards her. Hesitantly, he placed a hand on her shoulder. He had been so scared of this at the start, of making her cry. Now that it had happened, he was scared she would never forgive him.

When Nef sniffled quietly and leaned into his hand, Xander gave up. Sliding his arms around her properly, he hugged her tightly against him. She smelled like her signature perfume and his shampoo.

"Oh honey," he whispered into her curls. "I'm so sorry. The last thing I ever wanted to do was hurt you. Feel whatever you need, but I'm not giving up on us. We're going to get through this, I promise."

Hot tears slid down his neck as Nef started sobbing, but Xander didn't care. He didn't care about anything other than the fact that Nef was nodding and pulling him closer.

Now he just had to quickly think of a way to make this work.

His words felt too good to be true. Possibly because Nef was busy focusing on how good it felt to be in his arms again, how much she had missed this man who had come to mean so much to her in so short a time. Tucking herself closer to his chest, Nef inhaled his spicy cologne mixed with the sugary sweetness of... mint chocolate ice cream?

Hiccuping slightly, she allowed herself two more minutes to silently drop tears on Xander's bare chest before she pulled herself together.

"I'm going to forgive you." She didn't care that her voice was small and watery. "Not right now, but I know I will. I just don't know how to get there."

"I do," Xander kissed her forehead. "We're going to start with a break."

"What?" Nef must have misheard him. How would a break fix things? Xander must have read her thoughts. Chuckling softly, he toyed with a curl.

"Let's have a break. Not long, just until the end of your exhibition. You'll have time to focus on it, I won't be a distraction, I'll sort out my... work, and then we can meet up and start again. What do you think?"

It was a sensible plan, but Nef couldn't help but deflate a little when he mentioned continuing to work. Her head may be in that post-cry fog but she could still read subtext — and Xander was still going to buy her aunt's museum. What else did she expect though? That he'd give it up for her? A girl he met only a month and a bit ago? They were barely official anyway.

Biting her cheek hard, she savoured the sharp tang of rust and metal. "It sounds like a plan."

Xander smiled, hope shining through his expression.

"I can't promise anything though," Nef warned. "I don't want to guarantee that after the break things will just pick up again."

Xander's smile fell, but he nodded seriously. His obvious dedication to doing whatever he could to win her back was endearing. Nef couldn't stop her small smile from breaking across her face in response.

"So... when does this break start?" Xander still had an arm around her, and his warmth was bleeding into her slowly. Nef didn't want to leave yet. She couldn't believe he had only just gotten back and they were now going to separate again.

Stalling, she traced a finger lightly along the inner edge of his pyjama pants, committing the shape of him to memory for the next few weeks. Sensing the change in her demeanour, Xander's grim determination transformed into something headier.

"Tomorrow morning." Scooped up effortlessly, Nef gripped the back of Xander's neck as he carried her towards the bedroom. Tomorrow she would let go.

And then spend the next few weeks deciding if she wanted to grab hold again.

CHAPTER 32

Shattered pottery instead of Nef's shattered heart was a small break from the torture of the past few days. It had been a week since her and Xander's discussion and although they had mutually agreed to go no-contact until after the exhibition, the silence was killing Nef slowly. She hadn't realised how much she had been talking to Xander constantly, and it was messing with her sleep schedule trying to stop herself from calling him before bed each night.

Gritting her teeth hard enough to trigger a migraine, Nef watched an employee — faceless at this distance because she had forgotten her glasses *and* contact lenses

— sweep up the pile of spilled soil and broken pottery sherds.

The exhibition set-up was hypothetically perfect but theoretically not. Every artefact had been lovingly designated a place of honour, each olive and laurel tree's location marked with a tag colour-coded to a piece of tape on the marble floor. Lighting was complete, but moving the trees into the building had quickly become some kind of extreme sports event.

A migraine well and truly began to creep over Nef, the familiar nausea turning her stomach. No stranger to these frequent stress induced episodes, she quickly rummaged in her handbag for some aspirin, which she promptly dry swallowed.

One more week till the exhibition. One more week to get her shit together.

Sighing through her nose, Nef was about to go help the cleaning crew when a hand on her shoulder distracted her. Turning sharply, she halted as Tiye's bright hair wrap and matching lipstick nearly blinded her.

"This is a good sign," Tiye smiled softly.

Xander hadn't been the only object of Nef's wrath. She and Tiye had had it out after Xander left, their harsh tears a result of both anger and the acrid smoke from burnt dessert. Living with someone, however, especially family, made forgiveness a much faster process. And Nef knew that her aunt at least had been keeping quiet out of shock and a desire to not interfere in her love life.

Still, their relationship remained tentative for the moment.

"How is this a good sign?" Nef groaned as she dropped her forehead onto Tiye's shoulder. Defeat coiled in her shoulders as she listened to the frantic hollering of workers as they tried to not drop any more potted trees. "If anything else breaks, I have to change my budget again. And what if I don't have enough plants here on time for opening day?"

"It is a good sign," Tiye repeated firmly, "Because if things do not go wrong now they are more likely to go wrong on the day."

Nef finally met her aunt's eyes as Tiye took her shoulders with both hands. "Come, little Magpie. Your vision is magnificent. The exhibit will be grand enough to rival the temples the very artifacts are from!"

Laughing weakly, Nef surveyed the hall again. She quickly sent a prayer to the gods, hoping for Aunty Tiye's words to bear truth. A small smile broke over her face as she imagined what Xander would say when she told him about the tree fiasco. It promptly faded when she remembered that she wouldn't be telling Xander anytime soon.

God, what she would give to talk to him. But she knew she needed more time. There were plenty of things Nef needed to sort out herself first — the exhibition being just one of them — before she could think about sorting out their potential relationship.

Maybe she would take her aunt's suggestion and see a therapist. Goodness knows that that could help with more than just her worries about Xander. And with the museum's recent sale, they could definitely afford it now too. Nef still couldn't decide if that gave a point to, or against, the man in question.

The sound of another potted plant shattering startled Nef from her thoughts. Cursing, she rushed over to help. Thoughts of Xander could wait — for now, she had an exhibit to finalise.

The thick glossy paper was embossed with gold accents, and Xander couldn't help but feel proud of Nef and what she had achieved.

Standing stock still in the hallway, the rest of the mail he had just collected loosely fluttered around his feet, forgotten in the face of the envelope he held. Xander remembered seeing the early designs for these invites, spread out in Nef's binder with neat looping calligraphy annotating improvements around the edges. Nef had been so indecisive, and the fact that she had chosen one of the designs Xander had favoured gave him a small flicker of satisfaction.

He hated not talking to her. Hated the other, smaller handwritten note from Professor Perez that had come with the invite: a warning that Tiye had sent him the invitation to Nef's exhibit without her knowledge, but that she hoped he would come regardless of what was happening between them. If not for Nef, Tiye had argued, then as an honoured guest due to his new role as owner of said museum.

Xander ran his hands through his hair with a deep sigh. Never in a million years did he think he would be in this situation. Xander stuck the invite to the fridge with a magnet, then went back to his place on the couch so he could brood in peace.

Scrolling through emails that had built up over his week off, Xander's eyes skimmed over paragraphs, too distracted by thoughts of the exhibition. Of course he would love to go. If the success of the museum pointed to anything, Nef was a truly talented curator. Beyond supporting her, he would love to go just to see his death mask in its place of honour. But Xander had promised Nef space, and though the silence was enough to make him want to jump out of his own skin with impatience, he had promised to do whatever Nef needed. Anything, if it meant a shot at getting her back.

Over the next few hours, Xander managed to get through a few urgent work tasks before he officially gave up. Going back to his new favourite pastime, he pulled up his laptop and Googled Nef and the museum.

Articles popped up, most of the links already viewed. It was like torture porn, Xander mused to himself. These small news segments and videos of the exhibit's fast approaching opening day were more than just a way for him to stay updated about its progress. Every frame that had even a glimpse of Nef made his heart ache, yet he couldn't stand to look away. If the only way he could see Nef was through a screen, he would take anything he could get.

Xander could practically hear Asim teasing him, if the man could see him now. Pining for a woman he had only known for a few months, years after his vow to never have a long term relationship again.

But so much had changed with Nef. She made him feel... real. Solid. Like he could do more, was worth more, than his job. With a small jolt, Xander realised that he hadn't been treated that way in a long, long time. Had he really thrown himself into his work that much that he had become it?

Frowning, he shut his laptop with a sharp snap. He was the one who had initiated this no contact idea. He was the one who was waiting for Nef to decide their next steps. Which meant that he had decided his next steps months ago, even if he was only realising this now.

Lunging for the phone, he frantically waited for the ring tone to stop, heart in his mouth. He had to tell someone.

"Xander? What the hell man, it's almost midnight." Asim's gentle tone belied his rough words.

Glancing at the clock, Xander cursed silently. He'd been so caught up wallowing about Nef he hadn't realised the time.

"Sorry, Asim," he said sheepishly. "I just... actually I don't know why I called. I'll talk to you at work tomorrow."

"Nuh-uh, you don't get off that easily. You never call past business hours. Something's up, and I'm willing to bet the company its about a certain curly haired woman."

To stay silent, or not to stay silent. Xander could kill Asim, but he was also his best friend. Maybe, in a way, since that incident... Xander might have been holding Asim at arms length too. Somehow turned his no romantic relationships notion into no relationships at all. When had he last talked to his friends about his life without them having to forcefully pry it from him?

"Ok, so," Xander cleared his throat. "I think I want to try a long term relationship with Nef. Actually, I know I want to try it. I think I've fallen in love, and I should probably have told her that first before you, but I feel like I'm dying holding it in and I think I've known for a while, but now I've fucked everything up and I don't think she ever wants to see me again."

Silence.

"Asim?" Xander asked tentatively. "Are you still there?"

The sudden loud tone at the end of the line told Xander Asim had hung up. Hurt flared behind his chest. His best friend had finally had enough of his shit. Serves him right for not being a better friend over the years.

Flopping back on the couch, Xander flung a hand over his eyes, self pity and self disgust warring in his chest. He was a mess. Pressure built behind his eyes, but Xander shut them tight and curled into a ball instead.

The sound of his doorbell an hour and a half later jolted him awake. The lights were still on, and the clock said it was almost two in the morning. Memories of his call with Asim and his realisation about Nef flooded back to his sleep deprived brain, and Xander let out a loud groan.

The doorbell sounded again, and Xander dragged himself to the door, muttering a string of expletives under his breath. Who the fuck was at his door so early in the morning on a Sunday? Swinging open the door with enough force to rattle the stained glass panes, Xander's jaw dropped when he saw who was there.

Asim was holding a large bottle of whisky and a tub of mint chocolate ice cream, a mixture of concern and bashfulness on his face.

"Shut up and let me in. I know we haven't done this since we were teenagers but it's been years since you've said that many words to me at once, let alone about a woman, and I'll be damned if I let my best friend wallow alone without the proper goods."

Numb with shock, Xander opened the door wider and let his friend in. Asim passed with a clap on his shoulder, before heading straight to the kitchen to hunt for whisky glasses. Following silently, Xander watched his friend rummage around his cupboards for a few minutes before he found the desired glasses and some bowls for the ice cream.

"Still your favourite, right?" Asim nodded at the mint chocolate scoops he was piling into a mountain.

Xander nodded, not trusting himself to say anything without his voice cracking embarrassingly. His friend had come for him. He would never say it, and he knew Asim would never expect him to say it, but he was grateful beyond words.

With a dramatic flourish, Asim placed the bowl in front of him at last. Leaning on his elbows at the island, he placed his head in his hands and gave Xander a meaningful look.

"Alright, my friend. Talk."

CHAPTER 33

Everything was perfect. Finally.

Nef gave up her spot of honour where she had been standing before the museum's entrance, greeting people with a gracious, albeit forced, smile. She wore the same purple dress she had worn months ago at that gala with Xander, and every step she took made the material swish seductively over the marble floors. Sweeping through the doors to the exhibition wing, she revelled in the muffled but powerful sounds of her heels as she strode over the red carpet. Guests and servers alike (the former dressed to the nines in various gowns and suits and the latter in traditional black uniform) parted like the Red Sea for her.

Nef's illusion of power was unfortunately just that — an illusion. Each step masked the weakness in her knees. The glass of champagne she snatched off a nearby server helped hide the fact that her hands were trembling. In the warm soft glow of twinkling fairy lights expertly hidden amongst branches of potted olive and laurel trees, Nef could almost convince herself that she was fine. Nerves? Never heard of her!

Coloured chiffon and silk suits pressed against Nef's arms and legs as she weaved between columns and busts to try reach the podium. She wasn't due to give her speech for another hour, but the simple act of standing nearby would make her feel calmer. She hoped.

Nef reached the podium without needing to stop and engage in small talk. Huffing out a relieved breath, she surveyed the room slowly, mentally going through her checklist: no more shattered pots, no visible marking tape, benches were accessible but not detracting from the surrounding artefacts, artfully balanced in glass cubes or on top of their own pedestals.

Ignoring the thoughts that had been whirling around her head for the last few weeks, Nef allowed herself a moment of pride at what she had achieved. She had planned — and now executed — an entire solo exhibition. Curated it, designed it, set it up, and now, presented it to the world. Successfully, if the amount of people present and their supportive chatter suggested anything.

The people invited to the opening night were as carefully curated as the pieces themselves: sponsors, minor celebrities, and socialites mingled amongst less prominent guests such as the mayor, some council members, and museum board members and alumni. All employees were also invited as official guests, to admire their hard work from the last few months. Hopefully, in addition to glowing reviews, tonight would be beneficial in finding her a new job.

Nef let out a soft sigh, gently fingering the corner of the stack of palm cards she had left at the podium for her speech.

Yes, everything was finally perfect — except for the fact that the man she loved wasn't by her side.

Deja vu hit Xander like a sack of bricks as he slipped between a group of finely dressed men, blending in with the crowd in his tailored black tuxedo. He could have worn any of his finer outfits, but tonight wasn't about him. And considering the person it was about didn't really want or expect to see him tonight, Xander felt that subtlety was probably a safer bet.

Tugging absently at the bright red tie at his throat, he took in his surroundings with a mixture of awe and guilt.

Nef had truly outdone herself. The hall looked like a vision taken straight from the pages of her binder. He could hardly imagine the amount of effort this would have taken — he knew Nef had been working hard, and he had seen her tenacity at his auction, but this? This was something else entirely, an incredible blend of curatorship, collecting, and finesse all packaged in a luxurious, historical wonderland.

This was what he was missing in his own work. The passion, the eye for design. He could buy and sell pieces better than most people, could likely tell you the value of an artefact with a glance, but putting together something to show it off? In such a cohesive, engaging way that had droves of people flocking to the opening night?

God, he wished he had been with Nef every step of the way. He'd have given anything to be able to see the look on her face tonight when she saw the results of her labour.

Speaking of the look on her face... lights were slowly starting to dim further, a podium at the far end of the room shining brightly like a beacon. Lit up by the spotlight was Nef.

Oxygen? Who was she?

Xander certainly didn't know, and as he locked eyes with the woman he loved, the woman who had pulled him from his vow against relationships, he didn't really care that he was probably suffocating. He'd die a thousand painful deaths if it meant that Nef would look at him for just a second.

Nef's eyes flared wide, but she hid it well with a gracious shuffle of palm cards. The room hushed to a soft chatter, falling silent when Xander turned and glared deeply at a gaggle of women still talking near the back.

"Good evening everyone, and thank you for coming! I'm Nefertari Garcia, and it is my pleasure and honour to welcome you all to my first solo exhibition: 'Glory and Grief'."

An appreciative hum filled the air as the title was revealed.

"This exhibit is deeply personal to me. As many of you know, this is the final exhibition to be presented at this museum, which for the past thirty years has been presided over by the illustrious Tiye Perez — otherwise known as my Aunt."

Nef launched into a series of thank you's and the presentation of various bouquets for her aunt and other exhibition sponsors.

Xander jumped like he had been electrocuted when his name was included in a list of those she was extending thanks to for their donations and contribution to the collection. Guilt flared in his chest again, settling heavily in his stomach next to the ever present bubbling of lust that he experienced whenever he so much as thought of Nef. He didn't deserve her thanks, but he also couldn't deny the flash of hurt he felt when she brushed over his name like he was just an afterthought.

Applause died down as Nef resumed her welcome speech.

"— so with the closing of the museum, with this final exhibition, I invite you all to find and face your own glory and grief in each piece, the same way that I have. Thank you."

The applause this time was rambunctious, echoing through the cavernous building as the lights brightened once again, drawing crowds to weave between artfully stationed pillars and statues. But Xander stayed initially frozen, locked in a staring contest with the most beautiful woman in the world. He shouldn't be here. He really shouldn't have come. Because now, if Nef didn't want him still after tonight, Xander really would never have another relationship again. She had ruined him, and he wouldn't change a thing.

Xander shuddered out a breath as Nef looked away first. Pain lanced his chest as he glanced away from the clear devastation written on her face. Clenching a fist to stop himself from doing something stupid — like reaching for her — by the time Xander tried to meet her eyes again she had disappeared into the crowd.

Turning sharply with a groan, Xander ran a hand through his hair, a deep auburn lock falling over his left eye with the movement.

"You came." The Professor's statement held a note of surprise. "I hoped you would, but I didn't expect it."

"I did," Xander cleared his throat and stood a bit taller, heart pounding in the face of his lover's only remaining family member. Flashes of the night he had last seen Tiye pulsed behind his eyes. "As a guest of honour… and for Nef," he admitted.

"Why Mr Turner, is that a blush I can see?" The smile in Tiye's voice gentled the teasing remark as Xander whipped a hand to his face, as though he could feel the blood rushing to his cheeks.

"It might be a blush," he hedged slowly.

Tiye laughed loudly, the sound so similar to Nef's it hit Xander like a punch to the gut.

"You're being very honest tonight, Alexander. I hope that's going to be a recurring theme going forward?" Large diamond studded hoops flashed beneath the colourful headscarf Tiye wore as she tilted her head questioningly.

If Xander was blushing before, he must look like a tomato right now.

"Yes Ma'am," he said. "I intend to be exceedingly honest tonight. And I'm sorry for how my actions affected you as well."

Xander sagged with relief as a wide smile split across the Professor's face.

"My dear, your actions gave me a hell of a lot of money, and a chance of freedom for our Nef. No apology necessary — for me, at least. Now if you really want to make the most of tonight, I suggest starting with the pieces my little magpie bid off you — they're over that way."

Xander followed the path of her finger to the end of the hall, where two columns, carved with hieroglyphs, towered slightly over the rest of the columns in the room.

"Thank you—" he trailed off as he realised Tiye had already flitted away, nothing but a flash of colour ducking through the crowd.

Making his way through the throng of people, memories slammed into Xander as he remembered the last ball he had been at, with Nef even in that same dress that drove him crazy. He'd do anything to have her back again.

Finally, he reached the end of the room, successfully evading several potted trees and various couples trying to snag the benches beneath them. The columns were engraved with various cyclical Egyptian prayers, invoking life, death, and rebirth in various patterns. Grateful for his lessons back in college, Xander easily picked out the names of some prominent deities and rituals, again impressed by the sheer level of detail and accuracy Nef had packed into this.

Coming to a stop in front of the first column, he admired Thuya's death mask, the gold and lapis lazuli dazzling beneath the warm subtle spotlight and surrounding fairy lights. If he squinted, it looked as though the queen of old was surrounded by starlight. Skimming the plaque below, Xander felt a glimmer of pleasure seeing his name in the credits for the piece.

Opposite the death mask was the second piece Nef had won — the scroll from the Book of the Dead. Xander lingered shortly on this one before turning towards the second taller pillar, shoulder height compared to waist height of the other columns, topped with a stone relief of hieroglyphics covered by a protective glass box. Admiring the sharp detail of each glyph carved into the square red stone, he finally allowed his gaze to drop to the matching plaque and translation.

CHAPTER 34

The sound of your voice is rich, full like the taste of date wine and I, drunken girl in a tangle of flowers live only a captive to hear it.

When Xander's brows nudged together and his shoulders tightened, Nef knew that he had recognised the poem. She was standing slightly behind and to his left, so he hadn't seen her yet, but Nef was close enough that she imagined she could just catch the scent of his cologne.

Her fingers physically ached with the desire to reach out and smooth his brow, but she distracted them by fisting the skirt of her dress until her knuckles turned white.

Xander shouldn't be here. Hell, Nef had shredded his invitation herself, then burnt each scrap of paper in her lavender scented candle that she kept at Sophia's place for whenever she came over to borrow the bathtub.

How the smug bastard got in was beyond her. He probably flashed his charming, Hollywood smile and made the security personnel melt enough to let him in. Bristling, Nef forced herself to release her dress, fingers cramping from the force of her grip. It's not like she wanted Xander to turn around and point that smile at her. She definitely didn't miss it. Definitely.

The devil on her shoulder whispered otherwise.

Biting back a growl, Nef debated kicking him out on the spot. It wasn't good for her nerves for him to be here, and she couldn't tell if she was more upset at Xander for showing up uninvited, or if she was more upset at herself for feeling grateful that he had.

Before she could decide which, Xander finally shifted, dragging his eyes towards the short description below the translation. Nef knew what it said by heart:

Love Poem, ~1300 B.C., author unknown. Dedicated to X, my glory and my grief.

Placing a hand on her chest, Nef drew in sharp jagged breaths that matched her pulse. Xander still hadn't noticed her, and she was dying to see his face, know what he was thinking after seeing this final piece of her collection. She knew it was selfish, but she had secretly hoped that the reminder of her love letter would have affected him more visibly — not that she had planned on him to see it at all, if the shredded invite hadn't been clear enough. Although cathartic, that had been a very brief outlet of grief and rage that she didn't want to admit she may now regret.

Deciding on the plaque inscription though had driven Nef to near insanity. In the end, she knew she had to include it. Xander was an inevitable part of this exhibition — of herself, not that Nef was brave enough to acknowledge it aloud yet. The whole point of not seeing Xander until after the exhibition (due to close in a month) was so that she'd have the time to sort out her feelings, decide if she wanted to try again with him.

But seeing him tonight... Nef was kidding herself if she thought she hadn't made up her mind days ago.

As though her very thoughts pulled his attention away from the relief, Xander finally turned around.

Nef froze at the same time Xander did, meeting his piercing gaze breathlessly. It felt like all the air in the room had been vacuumed out, along with the noise of the crowd. As Xander started walking towards her, Nef could have sworn it was in slow motion.

She didn't realise that she had also started moving until she stopped in front of him, close enough that her breasts almost brushed Xander's chest with each breath.

They stared at each other, and Nef knew both of their thoughts were written all over their faces.

Xander broke the silence first.

"Tell me to leave and I will." His voice was like gravel, and Nef knew he meant every word.

"Tell me to leave, to do anything, and I will do it. *Anything*. But I need to tell you something first."

Desperation bled into his expression, cracking the ice that had surrounded Nef's heart for the last few weeks. She nodded, a small dip of her chin that had Xander's shoulders sagging with visible relief.

"Not here though. Is there somewhere we can go in private? Please?" He looked so forlorn, so... hungry for her. The rollercoaster of missing him, hating him, and not really hating him finally caught up to Nef, and she melted even more.

Not trusting her voice, she nodded again and started leading him out of the exhibition, making sure that the other guests (especially her aunt) were too occupied to notice them. Once they were in the safety of the hall, Nef ducked into a deserted storeroom, locking the door after Xander.

Outside the glow and murmur of the exhibition, the small storeroom felt cold and empty. Crossing her arms to ward off the sudden chill, Nef leant back against a tall chest of drawers and waited for Xander to speak.

This conversation was inevitable, but having it sooner rather than later made Nef's heart skip when Xander opened his mouth.

"I'm in love with you, Nef."

Her heart stopped entirely. In fact, Nef was pretty sure her entire body had stopped functioning. A faint buzzing sounded in her ears, and her vision was blurry despite her rapid blinking.

Xander shuffled his feet, drawing her attention to the suit pants hugging his muscled thighs. "I'm more than just in love with you. I love you more than I ever thought possible to love someone. You upended my life, when I thought I would never have a relationship again.

You don't have to love me back, and I know I'm not supposed to see you for another month until your exhibition closes — and your exhibition is incredible, by the way, but *you're* incredible, and beautiful, and smart, and kind, and you've never put up with my shit. I never thought someone like you could even exist. And — fuck, I'm rambling, sorry,"

A giggle burst out of Nef's mouth and she quickly clapped a hand over it in embarrassment. She couldn't help herself; she was too nervous, Xander was too endearing, and she had never seen him stumble over words before.

"God woman, I'm baring my soul to you here and you're giggling?" The smile tugging at the corner of Xander's lips reached straight into Nef's chest, stealing what remained of her heart.

Nef giggled again, the sound turning into full fledged laughter that Xander soon joined in with. Somehow they had moved closer again, and she gripped his upper arm for support as she doubled over soundlessly with mirth. After a few minutes more of this, they finally straightened to face each other, Xander wiping away a loose tear of laughter as Nef gasped for air.

"What, what I mean to say is," Xander's chest was heaving, "is that I am head over heels for you, regardless of how you might feel about me. And I am so, so sorry for not telling you about the museum sooner. I will apologise every day for the rest of our lives, if you'll let me — and even if you don't let me, I will make this moment be enough for me. But I love every single piece of you without reservation or hesitation, and I... I just needed you to know that. From me."

"Xander..." What was Nef even supposed to say to that? She didn't think there were words in any language that could encapsulate the myriad of feelings crowding her chest. Forgiveness, longing, certainty that this was where she was meant to be.

Words were overrated anyway.

She didn't know who moved first, just that one second she was in front of Xander, the next she was pressed between him and the storeroom door and he was kissing her like she was his salvation.

It wasn't a neat kiss. It was messy, and sharp, a clash of teeth and tongues and nails dragged down his back, apology and yearning and a declaration rolled into a single, entwined breath. A question and an answer.

It felt like eternity before Nef finally pulled back, panting. Her red lipstick had practically transferred to

Xander's lips and nose and chin, and her dress was already bunching up around her thighs, Xander's leg wedged between her own.

"I love you, Xander. I have for a while. And I'm sorry too, for how I responded."

Xander swooped back down to catch her in a kiss again, and Nef melted into his arms once more.

"Does... does this mean that we can try again?" The raw hope in Xander's eyes made Nef tear up again.

"I would like that. A lot," she breathed.

The tension in the air turned heavier, and a keen awareness came over Nef as she registered just how closely she and Xander were pressed together. Xander must have noticed at the same time, the stiff outline of his arousal obvious against her stomach despite the thickness of her dress.

As he started rubbing gentle circles over the backs of her knees, her thighs, Nef started breathing heavily, warmth flooding her lower stomach. Like their kiss, she didn't know how it started, just that everything felt good good good and Xander was sliding in and out of her so easily. The sensation of being properly filled for the first time in weeks made Nef impossibly wetter, and she savoured Xander's low swearing as her pussy clenched around his hard sex.

The slight pain from the chafing of his suit pants against her inner thighs — pants that hadn't even been removed, just unzipped — was enough to send Nef tumbling over the edge, her orgasm crashing into her out of nowhere, Xander following behind her with a few rough pumps.

It had been fast, but it hadn't felt like a quickie. It had felt like coming home. Like love.

They leaned against the door for a while longer, stroking each other's backs an d arms gently, soothing away the pain and uncertainty of the last few weeks. Eventually, Xander zipped his pants back up and helped Nef tug her dress down and fix her lipstick.

"Well, that was one hell of a reunion." Nef let out another nervous giggle as Xander unlocked the storeroom and started leading her back to the exhibition.

"Don't get used to it," Xander shot back with a grin. "I never intend to lose you again."

EPILOGUE

It had taken a lot of communication and compromise, but Xander was proud of what he had turned his business venture into. No longer did he run auctions or excavations. Those, he left to Nef — his girlfriend, love of his life, and the primary curator and director of their museum, now co-owned between the two of them.

Over the past two years, she had slowly taken over his role, while Xander stepped down from his company, finally leaving it officially under Asim's control. The freedom he felt, the passion he found in running their museum was more fulfilling than he had ever imagined.

Better yet was their immediate success. Nef's temporary exhibition had ended up becoming a permanent one. The love letter remained prominently on display, and Tiye would bring her students on excursions to the exhibit to analyse the pieces and the way the show was designed.

Today would be the first time the exhibition would be altered, and the nerves were driving Xander insane.

"Is everything in place?" His casual stroll through the museum's entrance belied the thumping of his heart. Nef was out setting up for her auction tomorrow night, and he needed this to be perfect for her.

"Yes, yes, everything is exactly as planned my friend. No need to go prematurely bald." Asim flashed a cocky grin as Xander lowered his hands, where he had indeed been ready to tug at his hair — now neatly cropped rather than shoulder length.

Checking his watch, his stomach dropped as he realised the time. Swearing softly under his breath, he ushered everyone out with thank you's and promises to keep them updated about the new exhibit's success. Checking the lighting a final time, Xander breathed a sigh of relief when he saw that everything was in its place. He closed the exhibit's doors and moved back to the marbled entrance, ready to wait for his girlfriend.

Just in time too, because Nef's heels clicked through the doors a moment later, her cinnamon and citrus perfume floating towards him on the breeze that followed.

God, he would never get used to this. Even though they had been living together for the last year and a bit, even though he got to wrap her in his arms every night and kiss her good morning every day, the sight of this woman with her killer red lips and sparkling eyes would never fail to bring him to his knees with desire and gratitude.

"Honey, I'm home," Nef joked with a smile as she engulfed Xander in a hug.

"Hey, sweetheart," he murmured, pressing a quick kiss to her cheek. "How was your day?"

"Only a few hiccups, but you know what Aunty Tiye says."

"The auction will go smoothly then," Xander smiled warmly as Nef removed her coat, revealing a tight but modest white work dress that nearly made him drool.

Nef wrapped her knuckles against the wooden desk of the reception area. "Knock on wood!"

"Would it make you feel better to see the new exhibit that I can confirm worked out perfectly?"

"Yes!" Her eager nod squeezed Xander's heart as he led her towards the exhibition doors.

Xander watched her face carefully as they entered the hall, the fairy lights splaying over her curls and dancing over her curves. Delight morphed into confusion as her brows drew together.

"Xander... this looks exactly the same."

His stomach clenched and heat flushed through his body. Taking a deep gulp of air, he was proud when his voice didn't squeak. "Are you sure? Let me show you this new piece."

Hand in hand, he pulled her slowly through the room towards the very end, where Thuya's death mask and the love letter were still presiding.

Nef looked amused now, and it took Xander everything inside him to not just stop and kiss her right then and there. He had something important to show her first.

Coming to a stop at the death mask, Xander silently swept his hand out, gesturing for Nef to look around.

"Honey, it still is exactly the same." Nef spun in a slow circle, an eyebrow delicately raised.

"Is it?" Xander croaked. Clearing his throat, he slipped a hand into his pocket. "You should check the love letter, darling."

Smile spreading, Nef only looked slightly exasperated as she turned to the engraved red stone.

"See, it hasn't changed —"

Nef gasped, both hands flying to cover her mouth. She lent forward, reading and rereading the hieroglyphs and their translation on the plaque below. Turning back to Xander in shock, a silvery film covered her eyes as she saw him.

The floor was cold and hard but down on one knee, diamonds glittering in the ring box he was holding out, Xander didn't feel anything but hope and an overwhelming sense of rightness. Of love.

Opening his mouth to speak, Nef beat him to it.

"Yes, Xander. Yes, yes, yes!"

A million feelings crashed into him, along with Nef as she threw herself into his arms. Lying on the floor with his girlfriend — fiancé — on top of him, he started laughing.

"I," he gasped out, "I have a whole speech, my love."

Nef was laughing as well, tears flowing down her cheeks as she covered his face in kisses. Xander had never felt more perfect, more happy, in his life. And this was now just the beginning.

"Tell me later," she demanded, shutting him up with a deep kiss.

So he did.

ABOUT THE AUTHOR

Evelyn Astra is a pseudonym. Evelyn is an author second, and a postgraduate university student first. She lives in Australia, loves her family's dog (and her partner), and her favourite colour is red. You can often catch her reading steamy romance novels in between doing flashcards. This is her debut novel.

ACKNOWLEDGEMENTS

Wow. My first book. I've always loved books (duh), and while I regularly devour all forms and genres of fiction - especially the ~spicy~ kind - I never dreamt of writing of my own. The reason this exists today is because of the following people, whom I can't thank or hug tight enough.

Firstly: to Adam. I cannot express how much I love you, but I guess immortalising it in a book is a pretty good start (better than getting a tattoo, I think our mum's would agree). You encourage me and inspire me every day, and there's no-one else I'd rather go through life with. Thank you, for everything.

To Ruth, Suzie, Paige, Iris, and Marie: thank you for being my best friends, my soul sisters, my writing buddies and beta readers. I am so grateful for you all, and love you guys beyond words. Special thanks to Ruth - for editing, and for reading scenes aloud to Iris while I waxed your legs in your dorm room.

To Bar, my long-time chosen sister. I hope this brought you comfort and enjoyment when you needed it most. Thank you for always being by my side, and for your much-needed feedback of the first draft! Still impressed you called it from page one.

To Gracie - your friendship makes me feel luckier than your four leaf clovers. You are a light in my life, a source of courage, inspiration, creativity, and support, and one of my closest friends. Thank you for showing me how to publish, for wine and pasta in your kitchen, and for everything in between.

To my parents and siblings: thank you for supporting me always, through my studies, moving states, and beyond. I love you guys. Extra special thank you to D, for devouring the draft chapter by chapter and for not judging me afterwards. There is no such thing as TMI anymore (sorry not sorry).

To my dearest friends - you know who you are, but special mention to Isabelle, Jake, Loren, Bridget, Faith, and Anila, who knew about this book first and some of whom helped beta read. You guys may not all have been part of the writing, drafting, or editing process, but thank you for being the sweetest friends, and for your excitement about this book.

Finally, to you, dear reader. I would always read this part of the acknowledgements and feel so excited - despite knowing the author would never know I even picked up their book at all. But I get it now. You make this all possible. I am eternally grateful you picked up my book, and I hope you enjoyed reading this as much as I enjoyed writing it for you. Thank you.

www.ingramcontent.com/pod-product-compliance
Lightning Source LLC
Chambersburg PA
CBHW020910130726
47904CB00006BA/1812